# Pride and Passion

Fern Michaels

BALLANTINE BOOKS • NEW YORK

# 1

Everywhere she looked the bright Brazilian sun illuminated the pageant of humanity on the rough-hewn river wharf.

Hawkers were everywhere, crying their goods at full voice. Sailors mulled about from one stall to the other, quarreling about the prices and paying them all the same.

Beggar children followed the sailors, pulling on their sleeves or tugging at their trouser legs, begging for a sweet or imploring the men through gestures to visit and buy something at their families' stalls.

While merchants haggled over the prices, Indian women dressed in long skirts wrapped about their slim bodies vied for the best of the merchandise. All about was color and teeming life. It was the most exciting sight Marilyn had ever seen, a far cry from her native New England.

Marilyn Bannon took particular notice of the Indian women. They were lovely to her eyes: smooth dark skin, not black like the Negro, but a nut brown; great dark eyes and straight black hair tied at the back. They wore bright colors and patterns which enhanced their complexions. Marilyn felt pale beside them.

She noticed a few of the women appraising her, and she felt herself blush under their impertinent stares. A few of them spoke to one another, nodding in her direction.

Marilyn's traveling companion, Mrs. Quince, noting her embarrassment, translated their light musical language for her.

"They say you are beautiful; they call you the golden girl. They're quite taken with your looks, and I believe they envy you."

"How odd, Mrs. Quince. I was just thinking how lovely they are. I admit I was feeling quite pale beside them."

"Well dear, you know the saying, the grass is always greener . . . Come, I must inquire as to which paddle wheeler we will take to Manaus."

At the name of the exotic city Marilyn felt a tingle and a quickening of her pulse. "Manaus," her geography text had read, "a treasure trove of wealth and culture, glistening beneath the Brazilian sun. It was erected on the banks of the Amazon at the height of the rubber boom, deep in the mysterious jungles of Brazil."

Carrying her bandbox and lifting her skirts gracefully, Marilyn began to follow the tall, angular figure of Mrs. Quince as she hurried off in the direction of the low-slung buildings at the wharf's edge.

A small boy dashed past her. As she swung sideways to avoid colliding with him she noticed a tall, dark, hatless man staring at her. The boldness of his gaze was disturbing and she hurried after Mrs. Quince to escape his rudeness.

When she caught up with the stately woman, she could hear the clipped tones of Mrs. Quince speaking to her. Apparently she was unaware Marilyn had left her side.

"—you'll be delighted with the paddle boat. It's just what a young girl needs. Gaiety and music. Our paddle boats here on the Amazon rival those on your Mississippi for luxury and food and entertainment. This will be a chance to wear your loveliest gowns."

Marilyn smiled as she watched Mrs. Quince's pale slate-colored eyes light with anticipation in her sharp, leathery face.

After booking passage on the *Brazilia d'Oro,* Marilyn allowed Mrs. Quince to steer her toward the wharf. "We can have our trunks transferred to the *Brazilia* when we board."

They stood at the foot of the gangplank, waiting for the purser to validate their boarding passes. Mrs. Quince was engaged in a lively conversation with the agent when Marilyn again became aware of someone's observing her. She lifted her heavily lashed gold-flecked eyes to the level of the promenade deck and discerned the same tall, hatless man standing at the rail of the ornate boat. She quickly glanced away, but found her gaze being drawn to him. His white tropical suit reflected the glaring sun and she had to squint to see him more clearly. A tumble of dark hair ruffled by the soft wind crowned a square, tanned face. He was handsome, masculine, and apparently very interested in her. His gaze was concentrated on her face, and she could feel herself flush in reaction to his audacity.

Mrs. Quince turned to see Marilyn looking up at the ship.

"Yes child, aren't they beautiful?"

"What?"

"The paddle wheelers! Aren't they beautiful?"

"Oh, yes," Marilyn answered distractedly, "I've heard of the river boats on the Mississippi, but I have never seen them aside from pictures."

Marilyn watched the people boarding the steamboat. Her eyes took in the bright white vessel with its red-and-gold-painted rails. The smokestacks were painted a bright orange, and the gangplank itself was a bright green.

Anywhere else these colors would have been overstated, but on the graceful paddle wheeler they were exactly right.

A porter came and relieved Marilyn of her bandbox and she followed Mrs. Quince up the bright green gangplank to the promenade deck of the *Brazilia.* She held tightly to the hemp rope handrail as she ascended the slanting plank. She was still not sure of her "land legs," and she felt she would be more secure on board ship on her "sea legs," which she had learned to command over the several weeks' journey from New England to Brazil. She wondered vaguely if it were possible to become "land sick." She had certainly felt queer since her return to solid ground. She said as much to Mrs. Quince.

"Oh lord a mercy, yes child. I, too, am feeling the effect of our long sea voyage. We'll be much more comfortable aboard the *Brazilia*. Truthfully, I can hardly wait to arrive at my plantation where I can be at my leisure and take life slow."

Marilyn found it hard to believe the energetic Mrs. Quince ever took life at a leisurely pace.

They followed the porter to their adjoining cabins. The small dark man opened the doors and led them into a cool, dim stateroom, furnished in quiet elegance. The theme of the room was that of a casual summerhouse, all cool greens and pale petal pinks. A deep rose carpet accentuated the light color of the draperies. Hanging from the low ceiling was a glittering crystal chandelier properly scaled to the diminutive proportions of the cabin.

Mrs. Quince's stateroom was similarly furnished, save that the carpet was a deep crimson.

"They will do nicely, won't they? . . . Marilyn, do you hear me?"

Marilyn wasn't listening to Mrs. Quince. Instead her attention was directed toward the open doorway where she had glimpsed a tall figure dressed in a white suit. It had moved from the doorway just as she lifted her eyes.

"Excuse me, Mrs. Quince, did you say something?"

"I was just saying these staterooms will do nicely, don't you think?"

"Yes, very nicely indeed."

"Child, you seem tired. Perhaps you should lie down and rest. You'll feel more like yourself and you'll be able to enjoy the evening's festivities."

"Perhaps you're right. I do feel a little tired."

"I thought so. Why don't you go into your room and rest—I'll see to our luggage."

After awakening from her brief nap, Marilyn felt refreshed and found herself excitedly anticipating the coming evening aboard the river steamer. From all indications, it would indeed be enjoyable. Already she could hear strains of music from the distant orchestra.

She quickly made her ablutions and sat before the kidney-shaped organdy-skirted dressing table to arrange her hair. She had hastily placed her toilet articles on the mirrored top prior to taking her nap. Beneath the bevy of hairpins, ribbons, and dusting powder she spied her silver-backed hairbrush.

Lovingly she picked it up and held it to her cheek. Somehow it brought her father closer to her. It had been his last gift to her before he died. She once again felt the deep, aching gap in her life. Perhaps after a time it would narrow, its sharp edges becoming less jagged and easier to bear. She studied the back of the brush. It was heavily engraved. Her slim, oval finger traced the "Tree of Life," the name of the rubber plantation to which she was traveling. It was from this same plantation that her father had come by his wealth. Now it was to be her new home.

Twin lines formed between her finely arched brows and for an instant she felt as if she were moving through time. Her thoughts slid backward, placing her once again on the steamer ship which had brought her to this exotic land.

The wind had been blowing gently, rustling the sheaf of papers she had carried with her to the mid-deck. Settled in her chair, she attempted to make some sense of her father's portfolio. It had all been carefully explained to her by the family lawyers, but she had been so filled with grief that their words were only a jumble and the papers she had signed had passed beneath her pen in a blur.

It was there on the mid-deck that she had come across a ledger which her father had used for his personal journal. Leafing through the pages she found the ledger opened to the last few entries: those written just before Richard Bannon's death.

Melancholia brought stinging tears to her eyes and

she fought them back in an effort to read the neat, small script. Something caught her eye, some oddly worded phrase which she couldn't comprehend. She then turned back to the preceding pages and scanned the lines. Nothing really, some mention of dates and appointments, a few others about a purchase of French wines for the cellars. Here . . .

*Heard from old Farleigh's lawyer today. Suppose the old codger finally retired and began to remember his old friends. Still, if what he tells me he suspects is true, I shall have to alter my plans concerning Marilyn's future. This will take prompt investigation.*

Then another entry, two weeks later . . .

*Quinton, Farleigh's lawyer, seems to know what he is talking about. The evidence certainly would seem to point to that . . . Still, I can not believe Carlyle would be guilty of such a dastardly action. It is not indicative of the young boy I once knew . . . Am waiting to hear from Quinton again!*

Another entry, a month later . . .

*Yes it is true . . . Carlyle has not abided by my wishes to comply with Princess Isabel's* Ventre Livre *law and I will not condone his actions. From recent correspondence with him and from other sources which have come to my attention, I tend to believe Quinton's accusations. This is not all; from searching my memory, I seem to remember my dear friend, Carlyle Newsome, Sr. complaining to me of his son. Something about the boy cruelly beating a slave to death. There was some talk of disinheriting the boy . . .*

And among the last entries . . .

*More and more I search the past; now I am
quite convinced Carlyle was responsible. I must arrange for a major upheaval in my plans for Marilyn. I am going to dissolve my holdings in the Tree
of Life and let Carlyle Newsome be damned!*

Marilyn couldn't understand what she had uncovered
in the ledger, and it was too late to do anything about it
anyway. She was already on her way to the Tree of Life.
Richard Bannon had died before he had had a chance to
withdraw from the plantation. She pushed the chilling
phrase which she had read in the ledger away from her
thoughts. Father had always been overprotective; still,
something was amiss.

Rifling through her bandbox now to find a fresh length
of ribbon, she came across the letter which Carlyle Newsome had sent her upon the news of her father's death. She
knew its flowery phrases by rote.

*My dear Marilyn,*
*I am much saddened by the news of your fa-
ther's death. I know his passing is a great burden to
you. I can only offer you my sincerest condolences
in your time of grief.*

*Your father was a much valued business partner
and greatly respected and honored by my father,
Carlyle Newsome, Sr. I remember having met your
father only once, when I was but a boy.*

*In correspondence with him, he asked me to al-
low him to appoint me your guardian in such an
event as this, his passing.*

*This letter is to extend to you a warm invitation
to the Tree of Life. It will be your home.*

*Enclosed are sailing dates for steamships leaving
New England, also instructions for your travel.*

*If you can arrange to book passage on the Victo-
ria, you will have the pleasurable company of Mrs.
Rosalie Quince, who is returning to Brazil. She will
bring you as far as the Tree of Life. Her own plantation is but ten miles from ours.*

*My sons, Carl and Jamie, extend their condol-
ences and wish you a safe, speedy journey.*
                          *My sincerest wishes,*
                          *Carlyle Newsome*

Mrs. Quince had proved to be a godsend. Not only
was her cheerful demeanor healing for the young girl's
wounds, but also her natural maternal spirit filled a
void in Marilyn's past and made the future seem less in-
secure.

The knowledge that Mrs. Quince lived on a neighboring plantation was a comfort. Marilyn did not know how
she could be happy in the strange land of Brazil with its
hot and humid climate. She dearly loved the small New
England town from which she came. But she had made
a resolution to try. She owed her father that much. For she
knew it had been his dearest wish that she go to his best
friend's son at the plantation, regardless of any alternatives
he had considered in his journal.

In fact, Richard Bannon had had such a high regard for
Carlyle Newsome, Sr., that he had appointed his son as
Marilyn's guardian. And his last words had been to tell
her to make arrangements to go to Brazil. It would be
her home. Owning half of the plantation, she would belong there. Marilyn had no relatives in New England.
She had been a product of a late marriage, and her
mother had died soon after her birth.

Richard Bannon had never quite gotten over grieving
for his young and beautiful wife. As Marilyn grew into
womanhood, she reminded him of his beloved Marie in
appearance as well as manner. Tall and golden, Marilyn
was her mother's image and at times it saddened the aging
Richard. But his love for his daughter was unequaled
and he doted on her, always providing the best for her.
The best included an education in the fine arts and
logical thinking. However, in his endeavors to protect her
innocence and guard her from the evils of the world, he had
neglected to prepare her for a life without him and to
teach her independence.

Now the anxiety of meeting people and living with "the

Baron"—which Mrs. Quince informed her was the popular name for Carlyle Newsome—and his two sons preyed
on Marilyn's mind. She had never had to adapt herself
so completely. She had always been sheltered, completely loved and protected by her adoring father.

She finished dressing her hair in the popular style of
the day. Her coif of golden curls, pulled back from her
smooth brow Grecian-style, was swirled into huge coils
at the crown of her head. The style accentuated her
graceful, long neck and softly rounded shoulders.

Choosing a gown of fine silk in a dark amber color,
she held it close to her body and admired her reflection
in the long looking glass behind the armoire door. Its
rich, gleaming folds were perfect for an evening of entertainment. Excitement eliminated the need for rouge and
she applied only a touch of pomade to her full mouth.

Gathering up her reticule and cashmere shawl, she
stole a final glance in the glass. Unashamedly, she appraised herself: tall and slim, almost too slim; rich vivid
coloring; golden-flecked eyes. She smiled. She remembered Mrs. Quince interpreting the native women's chat-
ter and saying they called her the golden girl. She
thought perhaps she should feel conspicuous for her fair-
ness in a land where most everyone was dark complect-
ed, but she recalled the eyes of the tall, hatless stranger
on her and tingled deliciously under the remembered
admiration of his gaze.

Pulling herself from her thoughts, she turned away
from the glass and was about to knock on the adjoining
door to Mrs. Quince's cabin. From the other side came
a call, "Yoohoo, Marilyn. Are you dressed?"

"Yes, Mrs. Quince, I'm ready to go." The door
opened and there stood Mrs. Quince. A handsome
woman, she had chosen a deep burgundy silk gown
which softened her angular figure.

"My dear, how lovely you look. You'll turn every
head when we enter the dining room. I hope you are
prepared to parry the notorious flirtatious natures of our
Brazilian gentlemen."

They left Marilyn's room and walked onto the promenade deck laughing over Mrs. Quince's amusing observations about the amorous nature of the Latin.

The dining hall was full to brimming when they arrived. "Oh dear, I underestimated the number of passengers who will be having dinner here the evening of the sail. I hope we will not have to wait too long for a table. I'm famished," admitted Mrs. Quince.

Marilyn was quite content to wait, however hungry she felt. The dining hall was sumptuous, approaching the point of garishness. Deep red carpeting, gilt-edged picture frames of questionable taste, floods of gloriously gowned women and scrupulously tailored men graced the hall. Crystal chandeliers cast a warm glow over the tops of the tables, causing iridescent shimmers to reflect from the jewels worn at the ears and throats of the ladies. After the sterile efficiency of the freight steamer *Victoria* which had brought them to Brazil, it was a welcome sight to Marilyn's eyes to feast on the opulence and splendor of the *Brazilia d'Oro*.

A heavy-set, stern-looking maitre d' approached them.

"If you will permit, mesdames, it will be an hour before you can be seated at a table. Perhaps you would like dinner served to you in your rooms?"

Mrs. Quince turned to look at Marilyn to view her reaction. Seeing the disappointment on her face, she answered, "No, we will wait. However hungry I am, I would not care to disappoint my young friend on her first night on an Amazonian river steamer."

The maitre d's stern look vanished and he braved a small smile in Marilyn's direction. He offered Mrs. Quince a slight bow as he took his leave.

The music had started to play again, and Marilyn turned to see the orchestra. The musicians were seated on a dais above the main floor of the dining hall. They were attired in bright red waistcoats and black trousers. She was surprised to see that all the musicians were Indian. They played the popular tunes so well, one would have thought they were English or American.

A movement caught her eye and she lowered her gaze

to the main floor. There, seated in an alcove, was the same gentleman who had so blatantly stared at her earlier this evening. Suddenly, their eyes met and held. She tore her gaze away but quickly found herself stealing another look. He was on his feet and coming toward her. Inexplicably, her heart beat faster, making her feel as though the pulsing in her throat was choking her. Her eyes followed his hindered progress through the crowded room. He was no longer looking at her; he was looking beyond her and inexplicably her heart fell. As he approached, she noticed the tallness of him. Well over six feet, if her guess was correct. Tall as she was, she would only stand as high as his broad shoulders.

Mrs. Quince made a slight gasping sound behind her. "Why it's Sebastian. We're in luck!"

He gracefully climbed the four or five steps to the level on which they were standing. He smiled, white teeth gleaming in his darkly tanned face; his eyes, she noticed, were black—Indian black. "Mrs. Quince! I had not expected to see you until sometime next month. Had I known you were traveling on the same vessel as I, I would have invited you to join me at dinner much before this."

"Sebastian Rivera, whatever are you doing in Belém at this time of year? One would think you were too busy getting your rubber to market to treat yourself to a sojourn in the east. However, I am sure, never has one been so happy to see you as we are. The maitre d' informs us it will be at least an hour before he can seat us to dinner." At her last words, Mrs. Quince turned to Marilyn.

Sebastian's eyes followed Mrs. Quince's gaze and he turned to Marilyn and gave a slight courtly bow. "Marilyn Bannon, let me present to you Sebastian Rivera. Marilyn is journeying with me to the plantation, Sebastian."

"How do you do, Miss Bannon."

His eyes flashed at her; twin circles of jet bore into her being. She felt breathless and struggled for control. Never had she met so handsome and dynamic a man.

Regaining control, she answered, "How do you do, Mr. Rivera."

"Ladies, please do me the honor of joining me at my table."

Mrs. Quince, in the abrupt manner to which Marilyn had become familiar, answered for them. "I thought you would never ask. But I warn you, if you hadn't I would have invited us anyway. So it's just as well you did, Sebastian!"

The twin orbs of jet glowed at Rosalie Quince. "Based on our long acquaintance, I've no doubt you would, Mrs. Quince. However, let me assure you, the pleasure is all mine."

He offered each lady an arm and led them down the few steps into the dining room. He then made his excuses and apologies to the people crowding the floor and adroitly led Marilyn and Mrs. Quince to his table and seated them.

The conversation was lively, owing much to Mrs. Quince's jocularity and loquaciousness. The dinner of stuffed lamb and rice was delectable, and the wine Sebastian chose to accompany the meal was the perfect complement to the savory courses.

When the waiter came to take the order for dessert, Mrs. Quince uttered a small squeal of delight. "At last," she sighed. "Sebastian, I can't tell you how many months I've hungered for *clea'ho.*"

"I could well imagine, Mrs. Quince. I understand guava is not a popular fruit in America."

At this exchange, Marilyn looked quite puzzled.

"Dear Sebastian is referring to my passion for the favorite dessert of Brazilians, guava paste and white cheese. Do you think you would care to try some? Or perhaps you would like to have a Blessed Mother?"

"A what? A Blessed Mother? Whatever in the world is that?"

Sebastian and Mrs. Quince laughed, but at the embarrassed look on Marilyn's face they quickly abated their amusement.

"Miss Bannon, forgive my rudeness. Mrs. Quince and

I are enjoying ourselves at your expense I'm afraid. A Blessed Mother is what the natives call certain little pastries. They're very similar to French petits fours. The Indians usually serve them on religious holidays, hence the name, 'Blessed Mothers.' "

"Oh, I see. Perhaps I shall try a Blessed Mother, if you don't mind." Seeing the apologetic looks on her companions' faces, she broke into a mirthful smile.

"It would seem our Miss Bannon also has a teasing sense of humor. Mrs. Quince, I cannot tell you how happy I am to look forward to this journey up the Amazon. Thanks to Miss Bannon and yourself, I believe I am the only gentleman aboard who is so fortunate as to be honored with the company of two such lovely ladies."

"Sebastian, save your speeches for the dance floor. My aged feet have all they can do to stand the pressure of my evening slippers. Pray, do not hesitate asking Marilyn to dance for fear of leaving me alone at the table." Mrs. Quince pressed her hand to her lips to stifle a demure yawn. "As soon as I have finished my dessert, I fear it will be all I can do to keep my eyes open. Therefore, I shall see myself back to my cabin and entrust you to see that Marilyn is properly entertained. I have no wish to act as duenna, I can assure you. I have known you long enough, Sebastian, to feel it quite proper to leave Marilyn in your care."

Sebastian nodded. "I shall be delighted to act as escort for Miss Bannon."

He turned his eyes toward her and smiled. Somewhere within her something stirred, making it hard for her to breathe.

He had kept his eyes on her throughout the dinner, abating his appetite. What was he looking for when he peered so deeply into her eyes? Why was it so hard for her to keep her eyes from meeting his? What was this strange emotion he evoked in her?

The music began to play again. A soft haunting tune with which she was not familiar. Waiters busied themselves quenching the candles burning brightly in the chandeliers above the tables.

A huge black man, dressed in bright gaudy trousers and an orange silk shirt open to the waist, proceeded onto the dance floor and squatted, placing a pair of drums between his knees.

The flutist played a haunting melody, rising an octave above the other instruments. Suddenly, on the dance floor were two other blacks, a man and a woman, both dressed in flamboyant costume. They assumed a stiff, yet graceful pose and waited for the music to reach its end.

The dining hall became quiet; the diners waited expectantly.

"You are in store for a treat, Marilyn," Mrs. Quince whispered. "This is, if I'm not mistaken, the trio that has been taking Rio de Janeiro by storm. They're from Africa, and I understand they're quite a success. I suppose they're on their way to Manaus to play at the opera house."

"Shsss . . ." came a command from behind Mrs. Quince. A woman gestured with her hand and turned Marilyn's attention toward the dance floor.

The woman began to move, swaying her hips in rhythm to the music; the male dancer followed her lead. The man with the drums beat out a slow rhythm which became imperceptibly faster as the dance wore on. The music took flight, the flutist now reaching low, mellow notes and then soaring to unbelievably clear, high-pitched tones.

The dancers followed the rhythm, swaying, rocking, becoming faster till they were swirling together, holding each other close.

Marilyn had never seen anything like this. She had been to New York once with her father, to the opera and the ballet, but somehow she could not imagine even the sophisticated New York society of the year 1887 accepting these dancers at their ballet or opera house.

Her attention was attracted by the woman dancer. Tall and lithe, she was now arching herself backward, her expression one of ecstasy. The light of the few candles remaining was caught by the beads of perspiration on her upper lip and reflected from them as though they were miniature diamonds.

The melody and rhythm became heavy, surging to a rapid crescendo. The music stopped; the dancers remained absolutely still, a dramatic tableau. The diners were hushed. Marilyn glanced around and saw men pulling at their collars and women fanning themselves rapidly. Within herself, Marilyn felt a novel excitement. She turned her attention to her own table. Mrs. Quince appeared mesmerized by the dancers; she was staring fixedly at them. Sebastian Rivera was staring at Marilyn. His look was penetrating, probing. She returned his look. She felt beautiful under his gaze, warm and sensuous. This man did odd things to her; he made her aware of herself, of her beauty, of her womanliness.

Their eyes locked. Deep, deeper. He gazed, she felt, into her soul, and she welcomed him.

Sometime shortly thereafter, Mrs. Quince retired to her cabin. Marilyn and Sebastian spoke of inconsequential things and shared the enjoyment of each other's company. Along toward midnight, Sebastian acquiesced to the lateness of the hour and suggested a stroll around the deck before escorting Marilyn back to her cabin.

The night was shimmering with stars. The Southern Cross was clearly visible and Sebastian pointed it out to her. Silence fell over them and they were still and contented with each other.

"What are you thinking of, Miss Bannon?"

"I was just thinking that home in New England it is late December, and the full force of the winter is just beginning. Here, it is eternal summer. It's hard to imagine a world so big it can have two seasons at the same time. New England always seemed the world to me. Now here I am in Brazil on a riverboat sailing up the Amazon to a city I'd not heard of till a few months ago. Save for the blessing of traveling with Mrs. Quince, I know I would feel frightened and bewildered. She has made this trip a most exciting event for me."

"Yes, Rosalie Quince has that way about her. She sees the world through the sharp eyes of a child. Every day is an adventure for her and she shares that adventure with those around her."

"I know what you mean. When I first met her she put me completely at my ease. She is truly a great lady."

"In more ways than you know, Miss Bannon. When Mrs. Quince came to Brazil forty years ago with her husband, Alenzo, she braved fever and famine to work at his side in the wild rubber forest. Save for her strength and perseverance, Mr. Quince is the first to admit, he would have turned away from Brazil to find his fortune elsewhere. From wilderness, and a thatched-roof hut, she and Mr. Quince carved a civilization out of the jungle. It was she who induced the Catholic missionaries to come to the wilds of the rubber forests to educate the Indians. It was she who founded the first hospital for Negroes and Indians. Manaus looks upon her as the grande dame of its society, and a dinner party during the social season is not a true success unless she puts in an appearance.

"Rosalie Quince has worked hard all her life, and sometimes I think it rankles her to have so much leisure time on her hands. Still, I think if she had the opportunity, she would gladly wrap her head in a cloth and work in the fields alongside her Indians as she once did. Mrs. Quince is a remarkable woman, and all who know her pay homage to her zest for life, absolute honesty, and integrity. I, for one, consider myself fortunate to know her and be recognized by her."

"I'm glad you have told me this about Mrs. Quince, Mr. Rivera. She never would have revealed it herself, although I must admit I have guessed at what you have told me. Only a woman who has known hardship can have the capacity for unselfish understanding. And this I have found in Mrs. Quince. I've been the beneficiary of her maternal instincts. I've felt she has privileged me by substituting me for her daughter Suzanne."

"You are correct in considering yourself privileged. Tell me, how did she find Suzanne when she went to America?"

"Very well, I think, though I know she misses Suzanne sorely."

Due to the slight breeze and the dampness of the night air Marilyn gave an involuntary shiver.

Sebastian took notice of this and gently arranged her shawl closer about her shoulders.

"Now I must take you to your cabin. I couldn't bear to have you ill for the remainder of the sail and be deprived of your companionship."

At his words, Marilyn lowered her lids, feeling that glorious warmth steal over her again. He placed his finger under her chin and lifted her face. In a deep, husky voice he said, "Forgive me." Before she could answer he brought his face close to hers; she could feel his warm breath upon her cheek and then his full lips grazed her mouth.

## 2

A current of emotions swept Marilyn almost to a swoon. Her body tingled and she felt herself drawn to him. She felt as though she were only half a person and he the extension of herself.

The brief encounter lasted only a second. Without another word he led her to her cabin and saw her in.

"Until tomorrow," he whispered.

"Until tomorrow," she answered, her eyes meeting his. Quickly, she lowered them, not daring for him to read the play of emotions he would find there. The door closed.

In the adjoining stateroom, Rosalie Quince smiled, heaved a sigh of relief, and turned over to find a more comfortable position in the canopied bed. In some small way, and much to her own amusement, she found she missed the lumpy and narrow bunk in which she had slept during her long journey on the cargo steamer. "Ridiculous," she chided herself. "However a body could miss that foul excuse for a bed is beyond me."

Even as she muttered the words, she wriggled slightly, seeking the familiar hole which she had worked into the straw mat that served for bedding on the steamer.

Silently, reverently, Rosalie Quince whispered her evening prayers before closing her eyes. She had lain in bed resting until she heard the door to Marilyn's room close; then, knowing the girl was safe, she felt able to sleep.

According to habit, she saved her prayers for her last thoughts. While still a young girl she had developed the knack of sorting her thoughts and mulling them over as one will do before sleep; then, when she felt all that could be done for the day was done, she would whisper her words to God and close her eyes for the night.

As she began her "God blesses," as she had done since she was a child, Suzanne's name came to her lips. Darling Suzanne, the only child of Rosalie's marriage. The journey to America, in spite of her cheerful demeanor, had been taxing and tedious. No longer young, Rosalie Quince nevertheless could not bear her daughter to endure childbirth among strangers. Even though the "strangers" were the girl's in-laws, Rosalie felt the need to protect Suzanne from whatever her new life cast her way and once again, perhaps for the last time, draw Suzanne close and help her through the pain.

It was not easy for Mrs. Quince to admit to herself that perhaps she had seen her beloved daughter for the last time. After all, she was not young, and she could feel the hot, humid jungle drain away her strength more and more, year after year.

Her arms ached for Suzanne, and she could again see the slim young girl standing on the wharf waving goodbye. It remained unspoken between mother and child, the fear of never again holding close one who is loved so dearly.

A sound from the adjoining stateroom shook Rosalie from her reverie. Aboard ship, Rosalie Quince had taken an immediate liking to her traveling companion, perhaps to defray the pain of being separated from Suzanne; nevertheless, Marilyn proved to be a young woman of warmth and charm.

Rosalie's maternal instincts, torn so savagely by her separation from Suzanne, were able to find refuge and comfort in the tutelage and protection of Marilyn Bannon.

Finishing her "God Blesses," Rosalie impatiently brushed a tear away from the corner of her eye, plumped her feather pillow, and fell back to render her keeping to the angels for the night.

Marilyn awakened leisurely. This had been the first night in several weeks that she had not felt herself cramped into a short, narrow bunk. She stretched her long, slim limbs, luxuriating in the feel of the fresh muslin sheets.

A feeling crept over her, one of happiness and anticipation. She had fallen asleep with thoughts of the lovely evening she had spent with Sebastian Rivera and Mrs. Quince, and now she looked forward to another.

She lithely jumped from under the covers and hastened to make her ablutions as though she could not wait to face the day. Humming softly to herself, she rummaged through her trunks and cases looking for exactly the correct costume for her first day upon the luxurious Amazon steamer.

Finally, choosing an aquamarine moiré silk morning dress, she sat before the mirror to dress her hair. She freed the thick blonde masses from their ribbons and began to brush the snarls and tangles from it.

It fell almost to her waist, cascading around her white shoulders. Every time she dressed her air, she reveled in its wealth and sheen. She could not help but remember when she was a young girl of thirteen. She had suffered from a fever, and the doctors had insisted on her being shorn of her locks. "It saps her strength." She could still hear the dour physician's voice and her father's murmured cry of dismay at this radical treatment. For months after that, Marilyn had refused to venture forth from the house. It was not until her hair grew back to a decent length that she allowed her father to buy her a frivolous bonnet and she shyly accompanied him for a ride in a hansom through the city park.

Now, as she dipped her fingers in the pomade and stroked them through her hair, she could bless the doctor who had issued the order. Her hair had grown back in a very short time, and where once it had been fine and silky, now it was heavy and glossy, obedient to the will of her brush. Marilyn considered it her most valuable feature.

As she was placing the last of the pins in her coiffure, Mrs. Quince knocked on the door. "Yoohoo, Marilyn, are you awake?"

"Come in, Mrs. Quince. I've just finished dressing my hair."

Rosalie Quince entered, still in her dressing gown. "Dear, would you prefer breakfast here in our stateroom or would you prefer to eat on deck with the other diners? Perhaps you would enjoy a view of Brazil as you sip your coffee?"

"That would be lovely, Mrs. Quince. I didn't get to see much of it yesterday."

"I thought as much. It will only take minutes for me to dress. Perhaps you would come into my stateroom and lace my gown for me?"

Twenty minutes later, Mrs. Quince and Marilyn were seated at a small table on the upper deck of the riverboat. Marilyn in her aquamarine gown had turned every head as she made her way through to their table. The richness of the moiré silk and the vibrant hue of aquamarine set off Marilyn's pale skin and turned her blonde hair to gold. Unmindful of the admiring stares, she followed Mrs. Quince and seated herself. Every nerve in her body was tightened to alertness. Then she felt, rather than saw, Sebastian Rivera approach them.

"Good morning ladies. I trust you rested well?" His

tone was light and casual; his eyes were sharp and piercing. Marilyn exalted in their uncompromising approval as he surveyed her.

"It seems, Mrs. Quince, I am in that unfortunate position in which you found yourself last evening. There is no available table."

Rosalie Quince, a smile playing about her thin mouth, lowered her head in a mock curtsey.

"Pray, Sebastian . . . I entreat you to join us for breakfast."

"I warn you, Mrs. Quince, had you not done so, I would have invited myself," he chided as he winked at her.

Remembering Mrs. Quince's words from the evening before, Marilyn laughed openly. "It would seem, Mrs. Quince, that Mr. Rivera has quite a memory for conversation."

Feigning annoyance, Mrs. Quince replied sullenly, "Yes, so it would seem."

Heedless of Mrs. Quince's mock scorn, Sebastian signaled to the waiter to bring him a chair to the table.

His poise and authority did not escape Marilyn. Once seated, he directed his full attention to his companions. "Tell me, Miss Bannon, has Mrs. Quince fully prepared you for the rigors of plantation life?"

Before she could answer, Mrs. Quince broke in, "The rigors of life in Manaus would be more the case, Sebastian, and you know it." Turning to Marilyn she began to explain, "I'm sure, dear, you've heard of the decadent society of Paris. Well, let me assure you, Manaus will soon rival that European city for its gluttony and distasteful displays of garish accoutrements. I, for one, much prefer the quiet, serene life on the plantation. I could well do without splendiferous-gowned ladies and men who tipple the most expensive wines. Were it not for the fact that I am sure it is only to flaunt their newfound wealth, I might accept it more gracefully. But this society is so ostentatious that it is actually perverse." Turning to Sebastian, "And the less said of it the better. Were it not expedient to maintain a townhouse for the sake of Alenzo's business dealings, I assure you I would not set foot in that devil's shrine."

Sebastian, who had heard this same point of view at other times from Mrs. Quince, smiled and commiserated with her. "I too prefer plantation life. And you are right, the less said the better. I wouldn't want to discourage Miss Bannon before she has had a chance to decide for herself."

"I assure you, Mr. Rivera, it would take much more than the evils of Manaus to discourage me in my opinion of Brazil." She half-turned in her seat to admire the view along the shore. "From what I've seen of your country, the only word with which I could describe it would be 'lush.' "

The waiter came and Sebastian ordered for them. Marilyn found it hard to concentrate on her plate under Sebastian's scrutiny. He watched her in open admiration. A table close to theirs was occupied by three gentlemen. Their admiring glances directed toward Marilyn brought a scowl to Sebastian's face, and he glowered at them, causing Marilyn to experience a delicious tingle within her.

After breakfast, Sebastian grudgingly excused himself, saying he had to meet with a gentleman in the lower lounge, but not before he made arrangements for Marilyn and Mrs. Quince to join him for dinner.

Marilyn watched his graceful movements as he took his leave. "Shall we indulge ourselves with another cup of this marvelous coffee, Marilyn?" she heard Mrs. Quince break into her thoughts.

"Yes, please, Mrs. Quince, and perhaps another wheat cake."

"Another wheat cake? Why you hardly touched—" Mrs. Quince broke off in mid-speech. She grinned at the blushing Marilyn like a cat that has just discovered a mouse in the pantry. "Yes, of course, dear, another wheat cake."

Most of the tables were empty by now, and the waiters were clearing away the debris left behind.

Marilyn attacked her coffee and wheat cake and was

putting the last crumbs into her mouth when Mrs. Quince said shortly, "He's a bastard, you know."

Mrs. Quince's proffered statement brought about the desired results. Marilyn choked on the crumbs.

"What—who?"

"Sebastian, of course." Mrs. Quince's penetrating look sought out Marilyn's opinions.

"Why do you tell me this? What concern is it of mine?" Marilyn tried to act blasé and was determined Mrs. Quince would not get any satisfaction from her scandalous remark.

All the while Rosalie Quince was peering into those gold-flecked eyes to measure Marilyn's mettle. It was a cruel thing to do, but Sebastian was dear to her and it would be best to see what stuff Marilyn was made of before he lost his heart completely to the golden girl. She liked Marilyn very much, "exceedingly fond" some of the sophisticates from Manaus would call it, but she liked Sebastian also. If the matter of his bastardy would put the girl off him, it would be best to know it now, not after, when real damage could be done to both.

"I only tell you this because I have eyes, and I wouldn't want you to hear it from anyone else. To be fair, before you make any judgments, I want you to hear me out.

"Society in the jungles of Brazil is much different from that to which you are accustomed. Here, we are swayed by what a man makes of himself; his beginnings are of little consequence. The natives and the Negro slaves so outnumber us English- and Portuguese-speaking people, it is only a matter of better judgment that we not hastily cast aside a member of our society for something as trifling as dubious parentage."

Marilyn's face flushed in embarrassment. To her knowledge, she had never listened to a conversation in which the subject was illegitimacy. She couldn't bring herself to question; Mrs. Quince answered her unasked inquiry.

"Oh yes, dear, Sebastian's mother was a native, an especially beautiful girl with a sweet disposition. She was devoted to her son until her death. As to his father, that is unknown. I doubt if even Sebastian knows who his father is. Although some say it was Farleigh Mallard, who left Sebastian a failing plantation and a barely adequate income—just enough to send Sebastian across the ocean to England to complete his education. When he returned from England, he took up the reins, so to speak, and worked day and night to make the plantation the thriving holding it is today."

"But why do you tell me this, Mrs. Quince? Don't you like Mr. Rivera? You seemed so glad to see him and your manner is quite friendly."

"Good Lord, child. Of course I like him. I'm quite fond of him actually. Even when he was a small boy, there was something intense about him, as if he were fated to be successful. The men also think a great deal of him. They consider him most honest and reliable. I'm glad to see he is finally accepted into the society in which he belongs."

"What do you mean, 'finally?' "

"Be it because of his Indian mother or just plain humanity, Sebastian's sympathy is with the Indian. When the plantation began to thrive, he freed his slaves and began to pay them a small wage in return for their labors. And labor they do. They honor Sebastian, they love him. He is their redeemer, their God here on earth. It is unheard of for a master to free slaves in these parts."

"Unheard of?" Marilyn was incredulous. "But my father was jubilant because Princess Isabel passed the law of *Ventre Livre*. I remember reading about it in my school books. Last year when the law was passed saying all slaves were to be free when they reached the age of sixty, my father told me it would be a matter of generations before all men in Brazil were free!"

"You are right, dear. In 1871 the *Ventre Livre* law was passed. This provided that all children born of slaves after 1871 would be free, as well as all slaves that belonged to the state or the crown. But unscrupulous plantation owners are only concerned with their rate of profit. They cannot find it in themselves to pay even a small wage for the work they have been getting for the price of spoiled food and a miserable thatched hut. Don't be shocked to come across deplorable conditions here in Brazil. Many of us are petitioning for the emancipation of all slaves. As of yet, the government feels the economy is too shaky. But if enough of us raise our voices, we will have to be heard. Sebastian is a great example for abolition. He owns no slaves and yet he yields the most rubber."

"How can these unscrupulous plantation owners keep the Indians at work? Surely they want to see their children free men?"

"Most certainly. The Indian's love for his children is unequaled. Yet there are those owners who say, 'If the child will not work in the field beside his parents, there is no room for him here. Put him out!'

"Parents do not want to be separated from their children, so they stay on and work for the owner, even those over sixty who might want to consider themselves free. Where can they go? Old and worn, who would give them work? No, they stay on at their plantations and labor till they drop dead in their tracks."

"What of you and Mr. Quince? Have you freed your slaves?"

"We have, those born after '71. But they are still too young to work in the fields so it has not strained our budget. And those old folk who are sixty and over, they have nowhere to go, so we give them light chores around the garden or in the dairy with the livestock, and they are grateful for the food we feed them and just to stay with their families. Besides, we treat our help most humanely. The conditions under which they live are far superior to those on many plantations.

"Sebastian is forever trying to induce the owners to improve the conditions of their slaves and raise their standard of living. He is indeed worthy of the adulation of his help. Kindness is his bylaw. He is the guardian of the downtrodden masses. Make no mistake, though; when he is dealing with the rubber traders he matches their ruthlessness. He is on the whole honest, but he is not to be put upon and cheated. He is wise and compassionate, truly a remarkable man." Mrs. Quince picked at a piece of lint on the front of her gown and said distractedly, "I had wished at one time he would be my son-in-law. But it was not to be. I can take comfort in the fact none of the other doting mothers of debutantes seem to be making much headway. I suppose it might seem strange to you that a mother might welcome a man born on the wrong side of the covers for her daughter's husband. But remember, I told you: society here is very different from that which you have known."

Marilyn smiled and gazed reflectively toward the water. She felt the light touch of Mrs. Quince on her arm. "Forgive me Marilyn. I wanted to tell you this in as kind a way as I knew how. I startled you in the beginning but it was for a reason. I'm proud of you for coming from so sheltered a life and accepting things as they are here. I can see it now. You will give the plantation life some sparkle. All the young men will be after you like flies to a honey pot."

Marilyn laughed aloud. *As long as Sebastian is the fly* . . . she thought secretly, and then blushed at the brazen thought.

That evening Marilyn dressed with extra care. Annoyed that her hair kept turning into curls unexpectedly, she tugged and pulled and combed and smoothed until she achieved the effect she wanted. A high coif, not *too* high but higher than that she was accustomed to wearing because she was so conscious of her height. But tonight she could be as stylish as she wanted for Sebastian was so much taller than herself. That afternoon she had buffed her nails till they had a soft gleam that enhanced her oval-tapered fingertips. The bath, which the porters on the paddle wheeler brought to her after many trips back and forth to the galley, carrying the heated water in great jugs, had been scented and taken leisurely.

Picking through her wardrobe, she choose a smoky rose silk gown with a puckering of ribbons at the bodice. "Simplicity itself," the New England dressmaker had sighed. It was of classic design, soft folds falling unhampered from the slightly elevated waist. A drop neckline left her arms bare and showed smooth, flawless skin against the muted color. Against her tawny hair, its contrast was striking. She picked up the ostrich plumes which were so popular and abruptly threw them back again on the dressing table. She would feel foolish and flighty wearing them. She knew they had been a mistake when the dressmaker insisted they would be a perfect foil against the simplicity of the rose gown. A simple pendant of quartz was all the accessory she felt she needed. All Sebastian would like to see her in. She did not take him for a man who liked to see women dressed in "gadgets," as her father had called them. As she sorted through her dainties to select a fresh handkerchief, she thought again of what Mrs. Quince had revealed to her that morning. Without a doubt it had cast some small shadow on Sebastian, but one which could easily be discounted. It wasn't for her that she felt dismay, it was for the man himself. What a strain he must have lived under, although he seemed to fare with it very well. Nevertheless, doubtful parentage was not exactly a boost to a man's career, and she was delighted for him that he had overcome its burden.

She stood before the mirror and studied herself. The gown was perfect, but she had doubts about the hairdo. Was it too high? Too affected? "No, silly," she told herself, "you'll do just fine. No sense trying to be what you're not! Still . . . no, it's fine," she assured herself. Before she could change her mind she hurried over to the adjoining door and knocked. "Mrs. Quince, are you ready?"

Sebastian was waiting for them outside the dining room. He was handsome in a dinner jacket of white gabardine with snowy frills on his shirt front. His deep tan and dark hair were in startling relief against the whiteness of his dress. He turned in their direction and saw them. His eyes fell on Marilyn and seemed to drink her in. Patience in dressing was well rewarded. He kept his eyes on her face as he bid them hello, and it was with effort that he drew his attention to Mrs. Quince.

With little conversation he led them into the dining room and escorted them to their table. It was the same one as the previous night and he explained that he had reserved this table for the entire journey.

"I wish we had thought to do the same, Sebastian. Were it not for you we would have been standing in that din waiting for a table," Mrs. Quince said, looking toward the doorway where a myriad of people stood waiting to be seated.

"I repeat, Mrs. Quince, the pleasure is all mine." This he said as he looked in Marilyn's direction. She felt her skin grow warm under his gaze. Why could this man make her blood race through her? Why did she find herself at a loss for words in his presence? Why was she acting like a schoolgirl instead of a poised young lady who had had the benefit of an education and profited from a finishing school? Why, when she wanted to be at her best, did she find her confidence in herself falter? But then, when he looked at her as he was doing now, her fears disappeared and she could feel herself preen under his attention. Her pulse would quicken and the very air she breathed would exhilarate her being. She felt herself fill out, a woman, nothing more, a woman. His kind of woman? She prayed so.

Sebastian only picked at his dinner, feeling himself nourished by Marilyn's presence. He watched her. Slim and lithe; poised, quiet. Not babbling on the way some girls did. She was gracious, almost queenly in her bearing. She made him feel a dolt. He, Sebastian Rivera, sometimes described as the most eligible bachelor in Manaus. He felt as though he had feathers instead of a backbone. Yet there were times when she looked at him, waiting for him to answer her question, or looking to him in conversation, when he felt he could be all she would ever want him to be. A man whose opinion she valued, whose words meant something. He believed she measured his words, listened to him. Not like most other women he had known, who patiently waited for him to finish his sentence just so they could lead the talk back to themselves. Or perhaps, while he was speaking, were wondering if their hats were on straight, or their hair falling out from some of those outlandish coifs they wore, or were fidgeting with their gloves, or worse, giggling in punctuation at the end of his every statement. This was a woman who was interested in him and what he had to say, what he was thinking. Nothing would ever convince him she was feigning interest. A man could tell those things. And in her deference to him, he found he weighed his words more carefully, pondered his judgments, considered his banter. He enjoyed himself, liked himself. He felt good to be with her, more a man.

After dinner Sebastian escorted Marilyn to the top deck. The night was sultry and from where they stood the sound of the great paddle wheel was a low whoosh as it propelled the luxurious boat through the dark waters of the Amazon.

The stars hung in the black sky, shining their dim, celestial light upon their faces. The moon at its first quarter was like an orange slice, precariously teetering in the heavens.

She breathed in the heavy scent of the tropical air. She became lost in the moment, entranced in the magic of the Brazilian sky, warm in the nearness of Sebastian.

He watched her as though from afar. Inwardly he groaned with longing for her and silently cursed himself for being at a loss for words. As he watched her, a breeze lifted itself across the water and blew against her. The soft folds of her gown were drawn against her, revealing the sensuous lines of her body. The breeze caressed her and wafted in his direction, bringing with it the scent she used. It reminded him of the earth, the sky, and the river he loved.

She turned to face him, somewhat embarrassed by her long silence, shy that her emotions were all too evident.

His expression as he looked at her made her feel giddy; she was aware of his feelings and reveled in them. The embarrassing silence became a silent understanding;

no words were needed. He approached her as she turned
to look out over the water. His arms slipped around her
and held her close. She could feel his warm breath
against her cheek and she pressed herself closer to his
chest.

Suddenly, his lips came down hard on hers, straining,
loving, wanting her more than he'd ever wanted a woman. And she was responding to him as urgently as he
hoped she would. In their ardent embrace, he caressed
her full, white breasts, feeling her nipples grow taut with
desire, feeling her body meet his with unrestrained passion. He kissed her hair, her neck, her eyes as she clung
to him, her heart pounding, knowing the feelings she
had were wrong, knowing they were improper for a lady
—wishing it would never end. He wanted to take her
right there on the deck, but knew he wouldn't. With an
inward groan, he let his passion subside and held her
gently to him as her breathing relaxed and she leaned
against him quietly, wanting more than his passionate
kisses—wanting his love.

A lifetime passed and she gave an involuntary shiver.
"You're becoming chilled. It's late. Come, I'll see you to
your cabin."

Silently, she acquiesced and allowed him to lead her
down the ramp to her stateroom door.

"I wish this night would never end," he said softly. "I
take heart that you will be near when we get to the plantation. Mrs. Quince's plantation is but a few hours
away."

"But I'll not be staying with Mrs. Quince," she said
happily. "I'm only traveling with her. No, I will be much
closer than her plantation. My destination is the Tree of
Life. I have inherited half the plantation from my father."

His arm which had lightly encircled her waist suddenly stiffened and he drew it away. Immediately she knew
something was wrong. She looked up at his face. Gone
was the warm, open look and in its place was an icy
stare. His firm, square jaw was set as if it were cast from

marble. His eyes were narrowed to slits and the look of hostility coming from within frightened her.

She began to speak, to inquire what was the matter. He did not allow this. Instead he made a perfunctory bow and wished her a good-night. Turning on his heels, he stalked away leaving her bewildered, humiliated and crushed.

After a night of tossing and turning, Marilyn arose feeling out of sorts from her sleepless night. Over and over she tormented herself with questions as to what she had done, what she had said to make Sebastian turn from her as he had. At breakfast with Mrs. Quince her eyes darted here and there, seeking a glimpse of him. Mrs. Quince noticed her lack of appetite and questioned the downcast girl.

Marilyn recapped for her benefactor the way in which Sebastian had left her the night before. Mrs. Quince put a comforting hand over Marilyn's and said, "I fear this has been my fault, child. So great was my desire to see you enjoy the voyage on the riverboat, I purposely misled Sebastian, and I fear you have taken the brunt of the results of my deception."

Marilyn watched the older woman gather her thoughts together and waited in suspense for the woman's next words. There was a slight lifting of the depression which she had felt. If Mrs. Quince could explain why Sebastian had left her as he had, perhaps it was something which could be amended. "Marilyn," Mrs Quince began hesitantly, "there is tremendous animosity between Sebastian and Carlyle Newsome. They greatly differ in their beliefs of how the workers should be treated. I know it seems a feeble reason but there's something else. Something I can't explain." Mrs. Quince lowered her eyes and seemed to measure her next statement. She lifted her head slowly and watched for Marilyn's reaction. "I might also tell you, for you will only see it for yourself, there is a very strong resemblance between Sebastian and the Baron."

Marilyn gasped and said nothing, her mind in a whirl. Then, regaining her composure, she said hotly, "But what has that to do with me? Surely Sebastian cannot blame me for his differences with the Baron! And as for how the slaves are treated, that is none of my doing!"

"I know, dear. It is most unfair. But you must understand; Sebastian has been at odds with the Tree of Life for as long as he can remember." Then Mrs. Quince sniffed and cheerfully stated, "Men are as difficult to understand as women, if not more so!"

All that day Marilyn caught no sight of Sebastian. She fervently wished to explain to him, to make him understand.

Shortly before dinner, a note was delivered to Mrs. Quince. It was from Sebastian, stating that he had left the riverboat when the paddle wheeler stopped at a riverport for water that afternoon. He graciously extended to the woman and her traveling companion use of his table in the dining room as he would have no further use for it and he knew it would make their journey more pleasant.

Where Marilyn had felt uncertainty and remorse over their brief relationship, she now felt anger. An anger so deep it cut into her, leaving her nerves raw and tenderly exposed. "You are a bigot, Sebastian Rivera, and I know it. If this is the way it is to be, then so be it!" she muttered under her breath.

She looked out over the water. The bright sunshine which had warmed her, brought life to her, now seemed clouded and a chill clutched her heart. She would not admit to herself that the sun had dimmed for her, that the emerald green of the Amazon had turned dark and murky.

## 3

Marilyn thought she could not endure another moment of the drive to The Tree of Life. The rough-corded roads caused the wagon to lurch first to one side and then to the other. Her body felt bruised and battered.

She sat in the back of the wagon surrounded by luggage and carryalls. Too exhausted even for sleep, she peered through the darkness trying to acquaint herself with their position. At last, giving up all hope of recognizing the dark shadows and resigning herself to the total blackness, she settled against one of the trunks and concentrated on the pool of yellow light which haloed through the thick humidity, throwing a feeble circlet of illumination upon the dry, caked roads.

Mentally, she counted the trunks and valises and carryalls which surrounded her. Her eyes came to rest on the largest of the trunks and she envisioned its contents. She saw herself, in her mind's eye, packing the simple gown she had worn on the riverboat, the gown which she had worn that last evening with Sebastian. Self-disgust washed over her. Why should I think about him? Why should I care? Mrs. Quince, knowing the hardship of the journey for Marilyn, silently cursed the fact that the comfortable coach which was to meet them had broken a wheel, and therefore they were forced to ride on the baggage wagon which her husband had sent to meet them at the dock.

Marilyn had been so quiet the last hour that at times Mrs. Quince was certain the girl had fallen asleep. Lifting the lamp high, allowing the yellowish light to fall on the girl, Mrs. Quince saw Marilyn seated among the luggage, wide awake, eyes staring into nothingness, a tight expression on her full mouth. "Damn you Sebastian for being the pig-headed fool you are, and damn you Rosalie Quince for trying to put your nose in where it doesn't belong!" she cursed. "It would have taken a fool not to recognize the attraction the two young people held for each other. What ever made you think you could play matchmaker? You old, foolish woman!"

Determined not to allow Marilyn to sit and brood, Mrs. Quince started a spate of patter and succeeded in prying a few half-hearted replies from Marilyn.

"We're almost here now, child," Mrs. Quince announced as the wagon suddenly veered to the right; "a few more yards is all."

Mrs. Quince tapped Marilyn on the arm. "We're here, my dear. Come now and the wagon master will help you down. One of the servants will fetch your baggage."

Marilyn nodded wearily as the kindly lady embraced her and kissed her good-bye. Mrs. Quince was going on to her own plantation several hours away.

"I'll send you a note in a few days time. Best get a good night's rest now." She gave Marilyn an affectionate hug.

"But aren't you staying here for the night?" Marilyn heard herself say. The weariness in her own voice surprised her.

"No, dear. Since I am this close to home I want to go on. I long for the sight of my husband, Alenzo, and I confess a great desire to rest these old bones in my own bed."

Strong arms helped Marilyn alight from the wagon. She swayed momentarily as she tried to stand erect. She could feel the blood coursing through her still cramped legs. Unobtrusively, she stamped her feet to hasten the return of circulation. While doing so she peered through the darkness to observe her surroundings.

A full moon shone upon the clearing around the house. It was one story high, a sprawling affair, quite different from the neat brownstone buildings found in New England.

The veranda seemed to encircle the house; white Cor-
inthian columns supported the porch roof and appeared
luminescent in the moonlight. Dark shadowy shapes
graced the foundation and a fresh scent emanated from
them. Tall trees leaned toward the house and rustled in
the warm, soft tropical breeze.

Gentle arms helped her up the stone steps to the veranda of the dark, silent house. The figure pulled a chain
and a bell peeled somewhere within. Moments later, the
door was opened by a tall, light-skinned figure holding
an oil lamp. Marilyn felt the dark figure of the servant
leave her side. The tall form with the lamp beckoned
her into the house.

Marilyn tried to open her eyes wide, but the effort
was too great; she did not care at that moment what
kind of an appearance she made. She was bone tired; all
she longed for was a bed and oblivion. In the morning
she would look at her new home. For the moment all
she had to do was remain alert enough to follow the tall
silhouette to her room.

"I am Elena, the housekeeper," the silhouette announced. She made a motion for Marilyn to follow her
as she held the lamp high to light the way down the dark
passageway. Marilyn needed no second urging. She followed quickly behind the regal back of the housekeeper.
The woman opened a door and held up her hand for
Marilyn. She supposed Elena meant for her to wait until
the room was lighted. Suddenly the room was ablaze
with light. Marilyn squinted against the glare. She hadn't
known what she expected in the way of furnishings but
this light Regency furniture was not it.

It was clearly a woman's room, done in pale beiges
and warm rose tones. The creamy lace bed hangings
wafted gently in the warm breeze from the open French
doors which were screened with nettings.

Feeling eyes upon her, Marilyn turned to face the
closed expression of Elena. "I'm Marilyn Bannon," she
announced in a friendly, weary tone.

"I have prepared for your arrival for many weeks,
Miss Bannon. I know who you are!"

Marilyn was surprised at the cultured, musical voice. She did not miss the coldness to the words, however. She looked into the dark eyes and felt instinctively that the housekeeper did not like her. She was too tired to care. She thanked Elena for the obvious care taken with her room and went to sit on the edge of the tester bed.

Elena watched the beautiful girl through cold eyes, then turned on her heel and left the room.

Marilyn reached down to undo her shoes and removed them. The small task wearied her so she lay back on the bed.

The next she knew there was soft sunlight streaming into the room. She looked toward the windows and noticed that during the early hours of the morning someone must have entered her room and closed the doors to ward off the morning heat. The sheer bed hangings were drawn against the bright light, giving the room a soft muted atmosphere.

A quiet knock sounded at the door and Marilyn bade the unknown visitor to enter. Elena strode through the door carrying a tray. Delicious aromas tantalized her appetite. Coffee! Marilyn sighed as she thought how good it would taste. She uncovered the plates and looked with interest at the thin, pink slices of ham, an egg, and a small pot of marmalade and fresh rolls crowned with a mound of yellow butter.

Elena looked at the tousled girl on the bed and let a smirk of rejection touch her lips. She spoke, however, in a quite civilized manner. "The maids will be here shortly with your bath water and to unpack your baggage." Finishing her brief statement she let her cold eyes linger a moment longer and left the room as quickly and as quietly as she had left it the night before.

Marilyn was bewildered by the coldness in the housekeeper's tone. As she ate her breakfast, she reviewed in her mind a conversation she had had with Mrs. Quince on the riverboat concerning the mysterious Elena. They had been sitting on deck enjoying the breeze blowing over the water. She had known that Mrs. Quince was trying to divert her mind from thoughts of Sebastian, and to please the older woman Marilyn engaged in conversation. The talk had come around to the servants on the Tree of Life and, of course, Elena.

"This is only gossip of course, but no one seems to know exactly where she came from. Oh, there have been many stories, but who knows the truth?" Mrs. Quince shrugged. "One story goes that she was born in the United States, that her mother was a Negress, a slave on some estate. Her father was a white man. This would explain her coloring, although to be as light-skinned as she is, it would seem likely that her mother was at least a quadroon. Elena is not at all black. In fact, she has a beautiful tawny complexion, large green eyes, and long silky hair, which she wears in two coils over her ears. She is truly a beautiful woman and she appears to have breeding. She carries herself like a duchess. She was a servant before the Baron's wife died, and since that lady passed on with the fever, Elena has managed the household for the Newsome family. At one time it was whispered that she was the Baron's paramour."

Marilyn fell back against the pillows chewing on the tender ham and thinking about that conversation. Mrs. Quince had certainly been correct in saying Elena was a beautiful woman. And now, in retrospect, Marilyn was surprised that the housekeeper was so young. She must still be in her thirties. She must have not been more than a girl when she came here to the "Tree."

Her train of thought was broken by the entry of four little Indian girls carrying in pails of steaming-hot water. One of the girls removed a screen from the far corner of the room and pulled out a large tin tub. The little girls poured the steaming water carefully into the tub and left the room. In a few moments they were back again with more water.

"Very good, girls," Marilyn said approvingly, as she rummaged in her carryall for the decanter of bath salts and poured in a generous amount. As she started to undo the bodice of her dress, four solemn pairs of eyes watched her. Marilyn looked at the little girls and did not know what to do. Surely they did not mean to help her!

"All right girls, you may leave. I'll ring if I need you." No one moved. Evidently they did not understand English. Well, what do I do? she wondered. No one was going to watch her bathe, little girls or not!

She took the girl closest to her by the arm and ushered her to the door. The other three girls stood rooted to the floor. The girl by the door had tears in her great black eyes. "What did I do?" Marilyn wailed. Solemn eyes looked at her. One plump little girl raised a fat finger and pointed to the girl by the door. "You no like?"

Marilyn was shocked. "Of course I like her. I just want to take my bath in private!"

"We help," the plump little girl giggled.

"But I don't need any help."

"We help," the girl repeated stubbornly. The little girls advanced toward the frustrated Marilyn. The child by the door stood mute, tears streaming down her face.

"All right, come here," she smiled. "You help too." The child rewarded her with a bright, toothy smile.

Before she knew it, her clothes were stripped off and she was submerged in the water. She was soaped and scrubbed till her skin tingled. The plump little girl attacked the golden tresses. "Pretty," she stated, the others nodding happily as they continued their scrubbing with vigor.

Marilyn wondered how long this was to keep up. Already she felt tired from their scrubbing. "Lord a mercy!" she muttered, parroting Mrs. Quince's favorite expression.

Her exclamation made the girls giggle; evidently they were familiar with the lady.

The first little girl held up her hand and said, "You wait, we bring more water." Marilyn sighed; where could she go in this condition? She smiled wanly at the girls as they trotted from the room. Fervently, she hoped the water was for rinsing and not more soaping. She looked at her rosy skin and winced. "I must manage to get a softer bath brush!"

The door opened and the giggling girls carried the pails into the room. They looked at Marilyn sitting in the tub covered with soap lather, their bright, dark eyes glittering in merriment. Apparently this is the part they enjoy best! Marilyn thought.

One of the children made a motion for Marilyn to get onto her knees, so that they could pour the water over her. "When in Rome, etcetera," Marilyn muttered. She did as instructed and as she felt the first torrent of water she heard one of the girls giggle at her repeated exclamation, "Lord a mercy!"

Marilyn choked on her own laughter at her own expense. Soon she was toweled dry, her long hair wrapped in a turban. Her skin felt tingly and renewed. Suddenly the plump little girl had a jar in her hands and she watched in fascination as each girl helped herself to a portion of the thick, fragrant lotion.

"Oh no!" Marilyn cried. What was the use, they would have their way. She let the girls rub her legs and arms. When they made a motion to remove the towel, she clutched it like a lifeline.

The plump little girl looked at Marilyn, her dark eyes dancing. "Lord a mercy," she chanted. Evidently this was her battle cry. Marilyn gave in gracefully. Her skin felt vibrant and alive as the girls massaged her gently.

Soon the girls had her dressed in a light, yellow-sprigged dimity that somehow was miraculously wrinkle-free. She was then ushered out to the wide veranda and gently placed in a rattan chair. The turban was removed from her head and the girls stood like bright, precocious squirrels. They cocked their heads first to one side and then to the other. They appeared to reach some sort of agreement, for the plump girl took the brush and started to brush out Marilyn's damp hair.

As soon as it was free from tangles, they sat down at Marilyn's feet and looked at her expectantly. Marilyn did not know what they waited for. She looked at the girls helplessly. The plump girl seemed adroit at reading her mind. She looked up at the sun and then pointed to Marilyn's hair.

"Oh, I see. You want my hair to dry and then you will fix it. Very good," she laughed. She wondered how she would look when these small children finished with her. *Possibly better,* she thought as she remembered their experienced fingers when they bathed her.

"What are your names?" she asked. At their blank expressions she pointed to herself and said, "Miss Bannon." Then she pointed to the girls.

"Nessie," said one, the smallest.

"Rosy," announced another, the one with the great black eyes.

"Blodgett—no! no!—Bridget," corrected the tallest child.

The last, the plump child announced, "Moriah."

"What strange names for Indian children. Where did you get those names?" Marilyn asked, smiling. Moriah giggled and Marilyn gave it up. However was she to communicate with these children?

When her hair was dry, Moriah jumped up to brush the long golden strands. She stood behind the chair while the others sat cross-legged in front of Marilyn. *The little vixens,* Marilyn thought. *They're the approval committee and they take their job seriously.* From time to time they squinted and nodded, mostly in the affirmative. Moriah kept up a running report and the girls again nodded. Nessie, the smallest, ran to get the hand mirror. "You see?" asked Moriah proudly.

Marilyn looked at her reflection. She was amazed at the artfulness the child had evoked. The light golden tresses were piled high on her head with a single curl falling over one shoulder. At her ears, tiny tendrils of curls were permitted to escape the pins.

They awaited expectantly for her reaction. She smiled and repeated their names. "Lord a mercy," she laughed and embraced the children. Unnoticed, Elena had entered the room and watched the scenario on the veranda through cold, green eyes.

With a loud clap of her hands the housekeeper dismissed the now quiet girls. They scurried from the room but not before the jolly, pig-tailed Moriah turned her head and gave Marilyn a precocious wink. Marilyn could not believe her eyes and had to stifle a laugh at the defiance of the little Indian. She liked the little girls.

"How old are the children?" she asked the housekeeper.

"They are ten years old, Miss Bannon. Were they satisfactory?"

"Most definitely. They are very experienced for girls so young."

"I have trained them myself," the housekeeper said coldly. "Master Jamie is waiting for you on the east veranda. The Baron and Carl are out on the plantation. They asked me to extend their warm welcome." If possible the cultured, musical voice was colder than before. "We dine at half past eight, Miss Bannon. Dress is formal." She glided from the room with a grace Marilyn envied. She felt awkward and schoolgirlish next to the regal Elena.

# 4

Marilyn followed the housekeeper down the hall and out to the veranda.

"You are Marilyn! I am Jamie," he said bowing low.

"I am happy to know you, Jamie," Marilyn said returning his smile. "I've come a long way to meet you."

He rose to full height. Handsomely tall and of muscular build, he was an impressive figure. His blue eyes smiled into hers and he impatiently brushed back a lock of springy, fair hair from his wide brow.

"It is my family's pleasure to have you here. I may call you Marilyn?"

"But of course. And I shall call you Jamie. Let us sit.

I wish you to tell me of the plantation," Marilyn said, seating herself on a rattan chair. "Why is it that you are not out on the plantation with the other men?"

Jamie looked momentarily angry. He became engrossed in rubbing the thumb of his left hand between the index and middle finger. He pulled himself to attention. "Father wanted someone from the family to be here to welcome you and to show you around on your first day. Besides they are dealing with the rubber merchants today and father did not want me aro—" Suddenly Jamie flushed and changed the subject. Marilyn pretended not to notice the slip of the tongue. Jamie then spoke of the plantation and the changes that had come to pass since he was a child. "Every year we have more rubber and better markets," he said. It sounded like he was repeating a much learned school lesson.

Marilyn spoke of the Indian girls and asked Jamie how they came to have such Christian names.

"That is Father John's doing. He is a missionary and he had converted some of the Indians. The four girls that Elena is training were born to Indians who are now Catholics." His eyes sparkled as he spoke. "They are wonderful," he smiled, "quick, bright, and eager to please. Especially Moriah. Is she not a quick little bird?"

Marilyn thought back to the precocious wink and agreed with Jamie.

"How many Indians are there on the plantation?" she asked.

"About one hundred and fifty; there are about the same number of Negroes."

"Do all the plantations have that many workers?" Marilyn asked, avoiding the word slave.

"Some have more. Sebastian Rivera has, in all, only one hundred. Somehow he gets more work out of the one hundred than we do with the three hundred we have," he said, frowning. "Of course you must have heard he gave his slaves their freedom. I am sure Mrs. Quince must have told you," he smiled.

Marilyn nodded. "Has the Baron considered doing the same?" she asked.

Jamie looked shocked. "He says he gets no work from them now. What would they do if they were given their freedom?"

"How long does he think he can hold off?" Marilyn questioned. "Mrs. Quince tells me it's only a matter of time until slavery is abolished, if Princess Isabel has her way."

"She never will!" Jamie roared, startling Marilyn to silence. Noting the shocked expression on her face, he continued in a quieter voice which he visibly struggled to control. "At the moment we are experiencing a bit of trouble with our slaves. We hear there is to be some kind of uprising. If so, that will be very bad; we have a large shipment to get out to the rubber traders on the next boat."

Marilyn nodded. She glanced at the table next to Jamie. "How beautiful," she said, admiring an array of wooden soldiers.

"They're collector's items," Jamie said proudly, handing her one of the brightly painted soldiers.

Marilyn admired the artistry of the small figure and commented on the fine detail. "How many do you have?" she asked.

"About seventy-six in all," Jamie said. "I hope to reach one hundred one day soon."

"I have never seen such fine soldiers even in the States. You must be very fond of them," Marilyn said.

"I am, Marilyn. They're my most treasured possessions. I've been collecting them since I was a small boy." Quickly he changed the subject. "Would you like to take a walk through the garden before the heat gets unbearable?" Marilyn nodded. "Later, after lunch, I will give you a tour of the Casa Grande." He extended a long arm and helped Marilyn from the chair. They walked down the steps, the smell of crepe jasmine heavy in the air.

Marilyn expressed delight over the abundance of sweet-smelling, lush flowers. Jamie explained how difficult it was to keep the jungle from creeping up to the door. "The lawn gets shorter and shorter every year," he laughed.

Within an hour the heat and humidity reached a soaring point. Marilyn felt light-headed.

"We had better go back," Jamie said, noticing her pallor. "I should not have kept you out so long. You must get used to the heat gradually." Marilyn secretly felt she would never grow accustomed to this strange land. She trudged behind Jamie on the narrow footpath.

Back at the Casa Grande Jamie rang for Elena and requested cool drinks. Marilyn sat and rested her head on the headrest behind her chair. The room was cooler and dim. It appeared to be a conservatory of some sort. She gazed around and asked Jamie what the room was used for.

"It used to be what my mother called her morning room. We moved her spinet in here after she died. Mostly it is never played. I come here sometimes, just to see if I can remember my mother. She died when I was two years old," he explained.

Marilyn asked no more questions as the housekeeper offered her a tall, cool-looking drink. She tasted it and her mouth puckered. "What is it?" she asked Jamie.

"Lime and papaya juice. We find it an excellent thirst quencher."

Marilyn agreed. A trifle tart for her taste but she supposed she would get used to it. "It is so pleasant here in the house," Marilyn remarked. "What a contrast to the heat outside."

"That is because the walls are more than a foot thick and the roof is tile. Would you care to see the rest of the Casa Grande?" he asked.

When Marilyn answered affirmatively, Jamie jumped to attention, ready to guide her.

The casa was laid out in the shape of a U; the walls of the casa surrounded a small courtyard paved with cobblestones and artfully landscaped with tropical shrubs and trees. Throughout, the furnishings were baroque in style, embellished by touches of gilt. Marilyn found she

was appreciative of her room with its Regency furniture.
The Baron's taste was much too ostentatious for her liking. Jamie pointed out different objects and she carefully complimented them, seeing how he was enjoying his
role of tour director. As they circled back to the morning room he remarked, "It's almost a perfect copy of the
original, down to the details."

"What original?"

"The original Casa Grande. Grandfather lived there.
When he died it burned to the ground. Father had this
one built soon after. The first casa was about a quarter
of a mile from here. Father didn't build on the old foun-
dations because he felt it advantageous that we be closer
to the river." Jamie was certainly enjoying his role as
guide. His speech about the old casa was spoken as
though he were reading it from a Cook's Tour pam-
phlet.

Lunch was served in a cool, dim room in the back of
the house. Marilyn was surprised at the quality of the
fine English china and commented on it.

"It was my mother's," Jamie explained. "We have
many fine pieces, as you will soon see." The lunch was
light and pleasant. A sweet salad of guavas and oranges
with pineapple, then some thin slices of cheese with wa-
fer-thin slices of bread and another glass of the lime-
papaya juice completed the lunch. Jamie escorted Marilyn
to her room for the siesta and told her he would join her
for tea at four and promised a horseback ride later.

Marilyn lay down with the thought of resting only.
Soon her eyes closed and she was sound asleep. The oppressive heat had worked its magic. Never before had
she napped in the afternoon. She awoke drenched to the
skin. Quickly she shed the damp clothing and made a
mental note to remove her outer clothing on the morrow
when she took her siesta. She changed into a light riding
habit and walked to the conservatory where she had
promised to join Jamie for tea. As she neared the door
she heard a low-voiced conversation from within. She
stopped and was about to retrace her steps when she
heard her name mentioned.

"Your father won't like it if you take the girl riding. You know he doesn't approve of your horsemanship, Jamie."

It was Elena. She sounded quite bossy and even petulant. "Why not wait till Carl returns and you can go together?" She was almost pleading. Marilyn stood quiet, listening shamelessly. "I am sure, Elena, that Marilyn is an accomplished horsewoman. You need not have any worries that she may fall from her horse or get tangled up in some poisonous vine. I will watch over her," he said coldly. Marilyn thought that with such a blunt statement the housekeeper would have thought herself dismissed, but she continued to argue the point, her voice lowered, musical cadence gone.

"If you disobey your father again, Jamie, I fear he will not order the new soldiers for you," she said firmly.

"Then I shall order them myself. I am no longer a child, Elena, as you well know. Let us speak no more of it. I intend to keep my promise to take Marilyn riding after tea— See that you fetch it immediately," he ordered imperiously.

Marilyn felt it time to make her presence known. She stepped back a few steps and stepped heavily on the tile floor, her heels making a clicking sound.

"I hope I am not late, Jamie," she said, entering the room. The austere housekeeper glanced at Marilyn coldly as she left the room. She returned almost immediately with two fine cups, a pot of tea and a plate of pastries.

"I think it is a little cooler, don't you, Jamie?" Marilyn asked.

"Yes, it usually starts to cool off around tea time. I find it the best part of the day. It's wonderful to ride as the temperature drops."

Marilyn had two cups of tea and several of the flaky pastries. Jamie seemed to have an insatiable appetite. He continued to eat pastries until the plate was empty. He smiled sheepishly at Marilyn's look.

"They are my favorite," he remarked, then burst out laughing. His laughter was contagious and Marilyn joined him.

"But not too good for the waistline," she said playfully.

"That doesn't worry me," he smiled again as he finished his fourth cup of tea.

"Is that your favorite, too?" Marilyn asked, laughing. He nodded happily as he set his cup down and stood up to shake the crumbs from his trousers.

Marilyn followed him through the kitchen area and walked out into the pebbled courtyard where two saddled horses stood waiting. Jamie helped Marilyn mount and they set off, Jamie in the lead.

Marilyn rode a dappled gray and Jamie a high-spirited chestnut gelding. He seemed to ride with ease. She wondered vaguely at Elena's warning, for it *had* sounded like a warning. Suddenly Jamie veered to the left and reined in the startled gelding. He dug his heels into the flank and the horse reared and pawed the air. Jamie continued to pull on the reins and the horse fought all the harder. She did not know what had happened. She hadn't seen anything on the ground to startle the horse. Luckily, her own mount stood placidly nibbling on the lush green grass. Jamie freed the reins and the horse quieted as he pawed the ground and nickered softly.

"What happened, Jamie?" Marilyn asked anxiously. Jamie's face looked contrite. "I don't know. One minute he was fine and the next he was in the air."

"You should never pull the reins like that; you only frighten him more," Marilyn said quietly.

"I know. He just frightened me for the minute. Come, let's ride a little further. See over there?" he said pointing a finger in an easterly direction. "That is the beginning of Sebastian Rivera's property."

Marilyn looked in the direction Jamie pointed and wondered where Sebastian was at this moment. She had not long to find out. Jamie dug his heels into the flank of the gelding and the horse snorted and took off at a gallop. Jamie did not have a good seat. He had been turned sideways to speak to Marilyn and evidently was not seated correctly as he turned.

The speed of the horse was frightening. Marilyn felt

helpless as she watched horse and rider plunge ahead.

Suddenly another rider came into view. He took in the scene and spurred his horse after the runaway gelding. Minutes later both riders came into view. Sebastian Rivera led the now docile horse carrying Jamie.

He nodded to Marilyn curtly. The way her white riding habit molded itself to her slim, supple curves did not escape him.

Sebastian choked out a string of expletives and proceeded to chastise Jamie for the foolhardy act. Jamie tried to defend himself but to no avail.

"Does the Baron know you are riding the gelding?" Sebastian asked quietly.

Jamie turned sullen and ignored the question. Sebastian shrugged and appeared as though he hadn't expected an answer anyway.

"Come, I will ride back with you to see that you get home safely." Their horses fell in behind the blue-black stallion that Sebastian rode. Marilyn admired the horse and the man who rode him so effortlessly. She knew that no other man would have been able to ride the huge black beast with the agility Sebastian displayed.

Jamie rode ahead, a sulky frown on his face. Marilyn rode next to Sebastian. She marveled at the ease with which he rode the huge beast. It appeared that the man and the horse rode as one. Marilyn kept her eyes on Jamie's back and did not attempt to carry on a conversation with the brooding Sebastian. He, too, wore a frown. What business was it of his where Jamie rode and what he did? And why did he ask if the Baron knew that Jamie was riding the gelding?

Suddenly Sebastian looked at Marilyn and spoke. "I don't think it wise for you to ride here in the jungles until you are more familiar with the terrain, and it would be best if you rode with an experienced horseman, which Jamie is not. There is no telling what may have happened to you." He spoke sternly, much the way an older brother would speak. Marilyn felt chastised. She flushed furiously and simply nodded.

"This is as far as I'll ride with you, Miss Bannon. I don't

think that the Baron would appreciate me escorting his son and his ward home from a ride." He again looked at Marilyn, swinging the huge horse effortlessly, and headed back in the direction from which they had just come. Slightly ahead, Jamie waited for Marilyn. His face was sullen. "I would not have allowed anything to happen to you, Marilyn; you know that, don't you?"

Marilyn nodded. She knew that intentionally he wouldn't have let anything happen—unintentionally was another matter.

Leaving the horses with one of the stable boys, they entered the cool, dim house through a side entrance. Elena came upon them as they entered the long hallway. The look of relief on her face was unmistakable. Relief for Jamie, no doubt, Marilyn thought sourly.

"You had no trouble?" she asked of Jamie. He merely shrugged. Elena did not bother to question Marilyn. The tall, stately housekeeper looked at Marilyn coolly, but spoke to Jamie.

"There will be heavy rains before the dinner hour is here. Perhaps you had best remove your soldiers from the veranda." Jamie's eyes lit up at the mention of his hobby and he went immediately to do her bidding.

The housekeeper again favored Marilyn with a black, malevolent stare.

"I do not want you to ride with Jamie ever again, Miss Bannon. Is that understood?" she asked frigidly.

Marilyn looked puzzled and asked, "But why, Elena? He did nothing wrong!"

"There is no reason for me to explain to you the why of anything. I have said you are not to ride with Jamie. Do you understand?" she asked, her eyes bright and piercing.

Marilyn murmured "yes" to the demand. She didn't understand, but she did mean to find out. She loved to ride, but if that pastime was to be curtailed she would find some other form of entertainment. She felt the cold eyes of the housekeeper on her back as she made her way down the hall.

Once inside her room she removed her riding habit and lay down on the chaise. She remained so, puzzling over the strange behavior of not only Jamie but Sebastian and Elena as well. Sebastian acted almost as though he were afraid for her to be with Jamie. Why? It didn't make sense. She wished fervently that Mrs. Quince and her mountain of information were here. A knock sounded on the door and the little Indian, Moriah, came into the room carrying a tall drink. She held it out shyly and Marilyn accepted it.

Marilyn patted the foot of the chaise for Moriah to sit down. The little girl looked frightened.

"It's all right, Moriah. I have given you permission. Come, I want to know how much English you know. Tell me, who teaches you?"

"Father John," the child answered shyly.

"I see. Do you also get to learn your numbers and your letters?"

The child again answered yes, "and Nessie too."

"What of Bridget and Rosy?" Marilyn asked.

"Elena says no," the child said, her face still and quiet.

"Doesn't the Baron have anything to say of it?" Marilyn asked.

"No, the . . . the . . . Elena says no," the child repeated stubbornly.

"Are you and the others to be my maids?" Marilyn asked.

The child nodded. "We take care of you," she said happily.

*And who takes care of you, little one?* Marilyn wondered. "Where are your mother and father, child?"

A frown crossed the little face. "My mother and father work on Regalo Verdad."

"Then why is it you are not there, too?" Marilyn questioned in disbelief.

"The Baron sold my parents to Mr. Rivera, but would not let me go. Elena wanted to train me for this plantation. Mr. Rivera is trying to buy me."

"How could they sell the parents and not the child?"

Marilyn felt nauseated. "Cannot something be done?" she asked. "And the others, Rosy, Bridget, and Nessie, where are their parents?"

"Also on Regalo Verdad. Mr. Rivera bought them all at the same time. They were all sick with the fever and the Baron said they were no good no more. He sell . . ." she floundered for the word . . . "cheap," she said triumphantly.

Marilyn's blood boiled. "How could this be? When was the last time you saw your parents?" she asked angrily.

Moriah held up three fingers.

"Years?" Marilyn demanded incredulously.

The child nodded.

"Well, we will just see about that," Marilyn actually yelled in outrage. The child cowered at the shrill sound. Instantly contrite, Marilyn cradled the small head in her lap. "I did not mean to frighten you, little one. I'm angry that this could happen to a child," she tried to explain.

"I cost many dollars," the child added proudly.

"Who told you that?" Marilyn demanded.

"I heard Father John say to Mr. Rivera." The round face puckered as she tried to remember. "Not enough money to buy me," she said. Marilyn understood. No matter how much Sebastian Rivera offered, the children were not for sale.

The child rose to leave. Marilyn, sunk deep in her own thought, did not take notice. "If I own half of this plantation, then I own half of all the slaves, and that includes the children." Granted, the casa belongs to the Baron, but the profits and the plantation we share equally. Then I should have some say in the matter." Rage and indignation welled in her, causing her temples to throb. They were only children, and try as she might, she could not accept the fact that the parents had been sold when the children were but seven years of age. She remembered reading somewhere that Indian parents were fiercely protective of their young. Then how did this happen? Perhaps they thought it best if they had a home? The children appeared to be well cared for. That, at least, was something to the good.

Marilyn opened the carryall that rested next to the bed. She withdrew the folded papers and glanced at them. She did not pretend to understand them. Perhaps Father John would be able to translate them. She knew they were legal papers testifying to her share in the "Tree." Now she needed specific information as to what her rights were to be.

She walked out to the wide veranda and picked up a dime novel she had tried to read on the voyage. She could not concentrate any better then she had on the voyage. Her mind was in a turmoil; it whirled in one direction and then another. Weary, she gave up and rested her head on the hard back of the rattan chair. From time to time she sipped the now lukewarm drink. She watched the sun go down and darkness descend on the lush plantation. The scent of the crepe jasmine was like a heady wine. It seemed to hang in the very air.

Eventually Moriah and Bridget returned to the darkened room and lit the kerosene lamps. The room was flooded with light. "Time to dress, Miss," Moriah smiled.

Marilyn rose heavily from the chair; she felt as though the burdens of the world were on her shoulders.

The small girls helped her dress, each quiet as though they sensed her mood. She looked in the mirror and was satisfied with the amber gown she had worn that first evening to dinner on the riverboat. She pushed back thoughts of Sebastian and adjusted a fold in the rich fabric. She thanked the girls, patted them fondly on the head, her heart heavy.

She entered the huge library where two men stood talking earnestly. Jamie appeared to be moping in the corner.

A distinguished-looking man in his early fifties seemed to sense her presence and turned toward the door. He studied her briefly through gray eyes. As he viewed her, she felt a faint blush under his apparently admiring gaze. Those steel-gray eyes swept her golden curls, strayed along her figure, and lingered on her face.

Marilyn stood transfixed beneath his gaze and in turn took her measure of him. Tall, slenderly built, yet strength of physique was apparent in his well-set broad shoulders. A shock of dark hair framed by white feathering at his temples caressed a shapely, regal head. His face, darkened by the sun, made his remarkable gray eyes appear almost luminescent. A full sensuous mouth, now smiling at her, revealed even, strong white teeth, accentuated by the small, carefully clipped moustache on his upper lip.

A woman finding herself so pointedly admired by such a handsome man could well consider herself flattered. Watching him, Marilyn felt an uneasy feeling come over her. There in the Baron's handsome face was a strong, undeniable resemblance to Sebastian.

"Welcome, welcome, my dear. The Tree of Life welcomes you. This is my son, Carl," he said, introducing the tall young man next to him. "And of course you have already met Jamie," he added fondly.

Marilyn smiled in return but felt her facial muscles were too stiff. She tried to relax but found it an utter impossibility. She felt as if she were on stage acting out a part in some play. She felt nervous and clumsy.

"Jamie tells me you went for a ride this afternoon," the Baron said quietly.

"Yes, you have very interesting terrain hereabouts," Marilyn said, waving a long, slender arm in the general direction of the outdoors.

"My dear, I would much prefer if you did not ride until you are more familiar with your surroundings," he said softly. Nonetheless, Marilyn recognized it for the order it was. She nodded her compliance and looked at Carl to see if he would add anything to the pre-dinner conversation. He merely sipped his glass of wine and spoke quietly to Jamie on the settee in the corner.

She quietly viewed him over the rim of a delicate sherry glass which the Baron had placed in her hand.

Carl was tall and sparely built, quite the opposite of the muscular bulkiness of his brother, Jamie. Dark hair slickly brushed back from an aristocratic forehead gave emphasis to his finely structured face and high-bridged nose. His pose, as he spoke to Jamie, was graceful and lithe, almost languidly elegant. It seemed to Marilyn that she was ensconced in a household of three dashingly handsome men.

The Baron spoke of the coming carnival and the festivities and how exciting they would be.

"It's the beginning of Lent. We'll go into the city for the opening of the carnival. We have a townhouse there that we keep. We stay there when the rubber traders are in town. We must see about getting you an appropriate costume for the ball." Elena broke into the conversation by announcing dinner. Without further words the Baron took Marilyn's glass from her and placed it on a marble-topped table.

She noticed that Carl and Jamie had already risen from the settee. Jamie rushed toward her, his arm extended, ready to offer it to escort her into the dining room. With a quiet grace, the Baron stepped between them and casually placed her hand in the crook of his arm. Jamie stood still, a sulky expression playing about his mouth. "Gentlemen," the Baron stated in a voice toned in a deep timbre, "I believe dinner is served."

It was a quiet meal. Again, Carl added very little to the conservation. He seemed, to the annoyance of his father, off in some other world. Jamie sat with lowered eyes, picking at his food. Marilyn found herself quite without an appetite. The creole shrimp looked and tasted delicious. The rice was fluffy and light. But it all had the effect of so much sawdust on her. The strong Brazilian coffee was served in the conservatory where they sat gathered near the small spinet.

"Do you play?" the Baron asked hopefully.

Marilyn replied that she did, however not too well.

Jamie suddenly came alive and begged her to play. She demurred at first but with the gentle coaxing of the Baron, she accepted the invitation.

She gently played love songs and sad songs. Jamie sat hypnotized by the soft sound of the music.

The Baron lounged in a brocade armchair, his head resting against its back, and watched her through lowered lids.

Carl stood by the open doorway leading to the veranda, a slight frown on his face. A faint breeze from the garden bore the scent of jasmine and was pleasing to his nostrils. The delicate music and the fragrance made him melancholy for the dark-haired Alicia.

Carl had no stomach for what he had to do once the girl stopped playing the spinet. He fervently wished she would go on playing forever. But there, that was further proof of what the Baron claimed was his foolish romanticism. Still, he knew he must follow his father's orders if the "Tree" were to be saved.

His thoughts wandered to Alicia and the desperate financial situation her family now found itself in. His mind rebelled; they were able to live quite comfortably, but the major portion of their wealth was gone—gone through bad business judgment. And now, her father was gone. An *accident*, the charitable chose to call it. But anyone knowing the true circumstances knew it for what it was: *suicide*. A further blot on the eligibility of Alicia, as far as the Baron was concerned.

Carl could still hear his father's persuasive voice. "The girl is not a good match," he had phrased it. "Carl, you must find a rich wife, one who will bring bounty to the 'Tree.'"

The "Tree," the "Tree," always the "Tree!" How could one measure the value of a damned lot of humid air, sodden ground, and a forest of rubber, compared to warm, sweet arms clinging tenderly; moist, fragrant breath against one's cheek; and warm promising lips?

"What better solution"—memory of the Baron's voice invaded his reverie—"than to acquire Marilyn Bannon."

When Carl questioned his father about the importance of a rich wife, the Baron admitted to him that he had been using Marilyn's money to administer the plantation and buy those luxuries which Carl also found enjoyable. The Baron's share had been left intact, free to gather a growing rate of interest in the banks. If the girl were to ask for an accounting, which she had every right to do, the game would be up.

He told Carl to marry the girl, then the secret would be safe, and the "Tree" would belong to the Newsome family.

Carl inwardly cringed as he remembered pleading with the Baron to forget such thoughts and allow his marriage to Alicia.

"Never!" the Baron's voice had roared. "Never will I permit a son of mine to neglect his duty to the family, to himself, to the 'Tree.'

"If you must have your precious Alicia, then have her. Take her, love her, keep her. Surely in their desperate circumstances, Alicia's family would invite a bit of assistance from you for something so trifling as the girl's virginity. Do what you will, but if I were to disinherit you—for any reason—do you still feel Alicia's mother and uncle would so welcome your attentions? I think not, my boy. They would hurry to move on to greener pastures. A beauty so fragile as Alicia's cannot be counted on to last past her mid-twenties. No, dear boy, however I see it, you are the loser." Then an icy gray stare descended on Carl and he felt as if frozen by its calculating coldness. Carl's heart had stopped. He knew his father was not making idle talk. Disinherit him he would. All things aside, even Alicia, Carl admired his father. Loved him.

The Baron had gone on to explain that Marilyn would never know how her monies had dwindled.

Carl watched the golden girl at the spinet. True, she was lovely and, he also thought, spirited. Would she have him if he did seek her hand? He loved Alicia, impoverished or not. His father's remarks about Alicia's character and reputation had incensed Carl to blind fury. Still, the fact that the Baron had overextended himself and needed his sons to stand by him in a time of trouble and uncertainty could not be denied. His father's sharp tongue concerning the morals of young women had been everyday fare since Carl was a young boy. He could not become too upset by further remarks concerning Alicia.

Suddenly, Carl's burden seemed lightened. How could he pretend to love Marilyn? If she had any intelligence, she would see through his scheme. She would then begin to wonder why he was pretending to love her.

Frantically, his mind sought for some other course. He knew it was to no avail. He had gone over the matter a hundred times. There was no other way if the "Tree" was to survive.

What in the world had the Baron done with all the money? The luxuries they had could not have used up all of her fortune. How could he have spent what was not his? Carl's hand wandered to his pocket where a note from Alicia rested, and his hand felt as though it held fire as his fingers touched the crisp paper.

He had sent a note in answer to explain that they had a guest at the "Tree" and he would not be able to see her till the carnival. In the note he expressed his deep love for her and promised the days would drag until he saw her again and held her in his arms.

He watched his father rise and applaud the girl's excellent touch with the spinet. A quick glance in Carl's direction, and Carl advanced toward her, offering his congratulations and inviting Marilyn for a stroll on the veranda.

Jamie made a move to accompany them, but the Baron called him back and told him that tomorrow he was to accompany him to view the rubber transactions.

This did not seem to impress Jamie at the moment. His mind and soul was still hearing the lovely music Marilyn had created. He must ask her to play for him again. He wondered if his own mother had played the same songs. Somehow he thought so. He had finally been rewarded by coming to the conservatory. He had always felt close to his dead mother when he was in the room. Now he felt even closer.

Carl and Marilyn walked in companionable silence around the the great veranda. Carl asked if she would care to ride to Mrs. Quince's plantation the following day. "In the trap, of course. But we will have to leave early to get a head start on the heat. We will return at night if that meets your approval," he added anxiously.

"Why thank you, Carl. I would dearly love to see Mrs. Quince again," Marilyn said happily.

"Then it is settled," Carl said briskly. "What do you think you would like to wear for the carnival?" he added.

"I have no idea," Marilyn answered truthfully. "What do the women wear?"

"I am afraid I cannot tell you, Marilyn, for that is the best kept secret of the year. The women guard their attire as though it were a state secret," he laughed. "The men, on the other hand, have a rather limited choice. You are apt to see ten or twelve of the same costumes on the men but the women's are unique. There is only one of each. The day after the carnival they start to ready their costumes for the next year. It is not unheard of for the winner of the ball to have spent an entire year readying her costume. There is a prize for the man and the woman. Mrs. Quince and my father are to be among the judges this year."

Marilyn listened raptly. She could hardly wait and decided to think about her costume this very night. She looked at the star-filled sky and suddenly thought of the heavy rain that Elena had predicted. "Elena said there was to be rain tonight," Marilyn said.

"Tonight?" Carl asked, puzzled.

"Yes. She told Jamie to take his collection of soldiers from the veranda because there would be heavy rains by dinner hour."

"I see," Carl said. "Well, I am afraid for once she was wrong, but, do not fear, in two or three days time the rains will hit us and then you shall be sick of them. They do nothing for the heat except to make it steamier and hotter than before.

"It is time we went in," Carl remarked as they found themselves before the French doors. "One of the girls will wake you in the morning and now I bid you goodnight." Quickly, before she knew what was happening, she felt a gentle kiss on her cheek. Carl turned on his heel and motioned for Jamie to follow him. Marilyn watched the brothers leave the room and a strange feeling came over her. It was as though something were off center.

There was no sign of the Baron. She picked up a lighted lamp and started down the hall to her room. She was surprised to see her bed turned down and her nightdress laid out. The little girls had been at work again. She noticed a large bowl of flowers on the small table by the bed. She wondered which of the four little girls had picked them. She knew it was Moriah. Plump little Moriah with the dark eyes and the fat pigtails; a beautiful child.

She undressed quickly and lay on the chaise with a pad and pen in her hand. "What shall I wear for the carnival?" She simply had no idea. Well, perhaps Mrs. Quince would be able to find someone who was skillful with the needle. Marilyn knew that if Mrs. Quince offered to help with the sewing herself she would have to reject the offer. She smiled as she remembered the messy stitches that so resembled her own. After a while she lay down her pen and thought of the events of the evening. Try as she might she couldn't pinpoint when the uneasy feeling began. Was it when she recognized the startling resemblance between Sebastian and the Baron? No, she didn't think that was it. She had been more or less prepared for it. Mrs. Quince had duly warned her.

Still, something didn't knit. Something was tilted. "Well, there is nothing you can do about it tonight," she scolded herself.

Lying with her cheek against the smooth, cool pillow slip, she once again pondered the off-center feeling. Too tired to think, she fell asleep. Her last thought was of seeing the four little girls in the morning.

# 5

The early morning ride through the jungle was an exhilarating experience that Marilyn knew she would not soon forget. The smell of the tropical flowers was intoxicating and the dew lay heavy on the lush green foliage, causing it to sparkle in the bright sun. Soon it would dry off when the light became more intense. Colorful birds shrilled and cackled as they flew through the dense forest.

Carl pointed out a large python that lay coiled and dozing in the sun. Briefly, he gave Marilyn a lecture on the snakes of the jungle, especially the poisonous ones —how they attacked and what to do if it happened. Marilyn shuddered and knew that if a snake ever bit her she would lay down and die. Where would she find a knife to cut the wound?

"That's one of the reasons why we do not want you to venture into the jungle until you know the terrain and can handle yourself. Never fear, it will not take long to learn the ways of Brazil." Carl smiled at her uncertain look.

They chatted happily and Carl gradually lost the worried look he had started out with. Marilyn was anxious to meet her friend and have a picnic breakfast at her plantation. *Won't Mrs. Quince be surprised?* she thought happily.

Soon they arrived at the Quince plantation. Mrs. Quince was quite overjoyed at the arrival of her neighbors. Much laughter and embracing occurred. Marilyn felt that Carl was embarrassed by such a blatant display of emotion.

"Come, my dears," Mrs. Quince cried happily. "I also have another guest for breakfast. I cannot quite believe my good fortune this day." Marilyn and Carl followed the aristocratic lady into the dim house and to the dining room. Seated at the table, his plate piled high with food, sat Sebastian Rivera. He stood and gave a slight bow in Marilyn's direction. She smiled coolly, surprised at his appearance.

"Is this not good luck?" Mrs. Quince asked happily. "Not one visitor but three! There are weeks on end that I speak to no one but my husband. I cannot wait for the carnival this year," she continued happily. "It will be a welcome change to live in town. I look forward to it every year."

Carl frowned at the sight of Sebastian Rivera. He wished he had known the man would be here. Now he had to go through the social amenities for the sake of Marilyn and Mrs. Quince. He despised the man. Actually, despised was too weak a word. He *hated* the tall, arrogant man of whom the other plantation owners thought so highly. He knew that his father and he were the only men who did not agree with the general opinion on Sebastian Rivera.

Sebastian stood to leave, his wide-brimmed hat in his hands. His breakfast forgotten, he thanked Mrs. Quince for her hospitality and nodded to Marilyn and Carl. His eyes glowed with hostility as he nodded to Carl. He strode from the room like a man with a purpose. Unhappily, Mrs. Quince watched him go. She hoped fervently that the news he had brought was not true. She knew that Sebastian was worried and her own husband, Alenzo, had been beside himself with the news. Rosalie Quince looked at Carl and decided to ask him pointblank. Shyness had never been one of her characteristics.

"Carl," she said sternly, "Sebastian came here last evening to tell of the rumor that there is fever on the 'Tree of Life.' Is this true?"

Carl looked shocked, whether at the news or the fact

that Sebastian Rivera was the bearer of the news was
not clear.

"There are a few sick Indians but I don't think it is
the fever," he said calmly.

"How sick are they and how many of them?" she
asked sternly.

"Four, I believe, and they have been off work but
three days."

"Is there no improvement?" Mrs. Quince persisted.

"I don't know. My father seems to think it is all part
of the rebellion they are about to stage. He doesn't believe they are sick."

"It wouldn't surprise me if they are. Alenzo has told
your father many times, and so has Sebastian for that matter, to clean out the lowlands and the marsh. That bad
air is lethal. The Baron promised but has never followed
through. There had better not be another outbreak of
Yellow Jack, for I feel I would not be able to nurse the
sick as I did ten years ago," she said ominously.

Marilyn listened attentively to their exchange. What
were they speaking of? Didn't the Baron take care of his
sick? Evidently not, if he sold the children's parents to
Sebastian Rivera. She would look into it the first thing
tomorrow and have a meeting with the Baron. If the Indians' welfare depended on the owners of the plantation
she meant to have a hand in it. She looked at Mrs.
Quince who appeared to read her mind.

"Carl," Mrs. Quince said, "why don't you go to the
stable and see the new foals we have? We need time for
some woman talk," she said bluntly.

Marilyn was thankful for her lack of tact. Carl stood
to leave, a look of chagrin on his face. Marilyn suppressed a laugh as did Mrs. Quince.

When they were alone on the veranda with the bamboo blinds closed to ward off the sun, cool drinks in
their hands, Marilyn started to question Mrs. Quince
about the children on the Tree of Life.

"It is sad, is it not? Unfortunately, it is true. The Baron does not treat his Indians and blacks humanely. The
living conditions are deplorable! Sebastian has been

trying for three years to get the children." Suddenly something bright green swooped onto the porch and settled on Mrs. Quince's shoulder. "Lord a mercy, Lord a mercy," it chanted in a raucous voice.

Mrs. Quince laughed. "This is my parrot, Bartholomo."

"Where is my sweetheart?" he chanted again. Marilyn laughed.

"At least he is someone to talk to during the day," Mrs. Quince said, laughing at herself, fine lines radiating from the corners of her sharp blue eyes.

"Tell me, child, how did the meeting go with the men at the plantation? What did you think of the Baron?"

"He has been most kind. I only saw him last evening. Carl has been very gallant."

"And what of Jamie?" Mrs. Quince asked, her tone suddenly sharp and her eyes bright.

"He is very nice and friendly. He took me horse-back-riding yesterday, to everyone's dismay. Evidently he is not an accomplished horseman. The Baron has forbidden me to ride with him. Jamie, I fear, was most upset. He appears to act like a spoiled child from time to time. But I like him."

"And the housekeeper?"

"She too has forbidden me to ride with Jamie. She takes too much upon herself, I fear. And yes, she doesn't like me. You were right, Mrs. Quince. I have tried to be friendly, but she is so cold I fear my attempts have been in vain. But tell me, Mrs. Quince, what is this about a fever on the plantation?"

"Sebastian rode here last night to ask Alenzo if he knew of any cases of Yellow Jack at the Tree of Life. So far, it is only a rumor. A rumor I hope does not turn out to be true. The last epidemic we had was also on the 'Tree' and it spread to here. We lost seventy-two Indians and forty-five blacks. I do not recall the number the 'Tree' lost, but it greatly exceeded ours. It's the Baron's fault. He has never adequately cared for the Indians. He expects them to work day and night and always to be hale and hardy."

Marilyn sensed Mrs. Quince's dismay over the loss of the slaves. She recalled Sebastian telling her of Mrs. Quince's long struggle to improve their living conditions. She also recognized Mrs. Quince's hostility toward the Baron and his indifference to the slaves.

The parrot suddenly set up a furious squawking. "The Baron is a nitwit. The Baron is a nitwit." Mrs. Quince laughed uproariously. Marilyn joined her as the great, beaked bird flew from its soft perch.

"As you can see," the kindly woman laughed, "he had heard it so many times he picked it up. When the Baron is here I have to hide him in the shed," she said, wiping her eyes on the hem of her skirt.

"As I was saying, child, if you own half the plantation, it is time you took a hand and a say in the running of it. The other plantation owners have stood still long enough. If another case of fever breaks out there will be trouble all around. We must get the rubber shipment out before the lowlands go dry. The rubber traders will be here right before the carnival. We cannot afford any delays at this time of year. And we don't want any lives lost unnecessarily." Marilyn nodded and spoke of her intention of looking into the matter in the morning.

Later, while talking about the coming carnival, they looked up as the sound of thundering hooves rent the air. "That is Sebastian. I imagine that he, too, stopped to see the foals before saddling that monster horse of his. Is it not magnificent?" Mrs. Quince studied the pose of nonchalance Marilyn affected. But her sharp eyes peered deep into the girl's face and saw there a shadow of pain. Immediately Rosalie Quince was remorseful for drawing the girl's attention to Sebastian.

Sebastian Rivera rode from the plantation as though there were a herd of wild beasts on his trail. Of all the bad luck! He had to run into Carl Newsome and the girl at Mrs. Quince's house! He frowned at the thought of Carl and the girl together, though why it should bother him he did not know, he chided himself. Just another pretty American face! All golden and soft. She wouldn't last long in this tortuous climate. She would soon pick up her skirts and head back to New England. The thought saddened him. She was a beautiful girl, and evidently Mrs. Quince thought highly of her. He shook his head as he spurred the great horse forward. He remembered her long delicate fingers and white creamy skin. She did not know what work was. She was probably from a wealthy family and had servants like his own mother to wait on her hand and foot. The thought of his care-worn mother caused him to grit his teeth. She had labored all her life just to keep him at her side. That was the deepest love there was. He had tried unsuccessfully to set aside all memory of his dubious parentage. A man is a man. And a man is what he makes of himself. He couldn't imagine this fine American girl with the golden hair acknowledging him as a man of his own. Proper parents and the proper upbringing would be all-important to her. Were she to know he was a bastard she would no doubt cut him off from her society. Yet, there was that small niggling doubt. She had seemed so different on the riverboat. When he had believed her to be Mrs. Quince's guest he found himself drawn to her, infatuated with her loveliness. But no, she was to live on the "Tree," part-owner in fact. He remembered an old adage and mumbled it under his breath, "Birds of a feather." He punctuated his distaste by biting the tip of a fresh cheroot and forcefully spitting it out. The Baron has probably already made plans for Carl to marry her, he thought bitterly. He didn't know why the idea should occur to him or why it should be any of his concern. Possibly they deserved each other. A thought came to him: last night at the dinner table Mrs. Quince had spoken to Alenzo of the fact that the girl had said she was part-owner of the plantation. Well, he would sit back and wait and see if she took a hand in things. He knew he could depend on Rosalie Quince to explain the conditions at the "Tree." He continued to ride as though the hounds of hell were on his trail. He wanted to flee from these thoughts. It was time for a trip into Para and the sloe-eyed beauty he kept in residence in his townhouse. He smiled to himself as he thought of the coming evening and the pleasure it would hold for him. He would deny to no man the fact that he liked the pleasure of a woman.

Back at the plantation Carl joined Mrs. Quince and Marilyn on the veranda and contributed to the talk of the coming carnival and the round of parties and the big parade.

"Do the servants go to the carnival?" Marilyn asked innocently.

"But of course. The carnival is for everyone. They have their own parties and entertainment, not as lavish as ours but they enjoy a good time."

"Tell me, child, where do you wish me to have the party for you? Do you prefer the townhouse or the plantation? I myself prefer the townhouse. Everyone will be in town as it is the height of the season. What do you think, Carl?" He nodded in agreement.

The rest of the day passed quietly. With the matter of the party settled in favor of the townhouse, talk ranged from parties to plantation life and the servants, Indians, and blacks. Mrs. Quince cautioned Carl again to warn the Baron on the living conditions of the Indians. And she asked whether the Baron had decided about the children. Would he return them to their parents at the Rivera plantation?

Carl shook his head and said the Baron would not part with the girls.

Marilyn looked from one to the other. "The children will be returned to their parents," Marilyn stated quietly and coldly. "I will not have that on my conscience." Both looked at her in surprise. Approval replaced the look of surprise on Mrs. Quince's face. Shock replaced the surprise on Carl's face. Marilyn waited expectantly for some comment. None was made. Instead Mrs. Quince announced an early tea—she knew the young people wanted to leave in order to arrive home before dark.

Marilyn's thanks for the lovely visit were effusive. Carl was more formal and more quiet than usual.

On the ride back to the "Tree," Marilyn had the feeling that he wanted to say something but did not know how to say it. Bluntly she asked him what was troubling him.

"Marilyn, I do not think you should make such a rash statement as you did to Mrs. Quince. The Baron runs the plantation and he will brook no interference. A woman has no say in the running of the plantation."

"Even if the woman owns half of said plantation?" she asked coldly.

Carl stammered as he again tried to persuade her to let the matter drop.

"Carl, I mean to see that the conditions of the Indians and the blacks are made livable and tolerable. I could not live with myself and take money from someone's suffering. I do not see how you, as a man, can condone it. Evidently the other plantation owners do not do this and they still show a profit and survive."

"It is the Baron's way and he has so far been successful. I would not interfere if I were you," he said quietly.

"Well, I am not you and I do mean to take a hand," Marilyn said sharply.

Carl let the matter rest and the remainder of the trip passed with both of them remaining silent. Marilyn's thoughts were of handsome Sebastian, and Carl's were on the impoverished Alicia and his love for her.

# 6

Marilyn dressed hurriedly and fidgeted while Moriah brushed her hair. She wanted to speak to the Baron before dinner. She wanted the matter of the girls settled and the accounting of her holdings. She felt nervous and a bit light-headed. She knew the meeting would not go well, as Carl, in his own way, had tried to warn her. Still she had to try. Her father would have expected it of her.

She waved the little girls away and lightly dusted her cheeks with rice powder. Playfully she put a dab on each of the little girls' faces. They giggled as they looked at each other.

Quickly, Marilyn left the room. The sooner she faced the Baron the sooner it would be over.

She entered the library just as Carl finished saying they had had a pleasant outing.

Marilyn tightened the muscles in her body. She walked over to the Baron and said, "May I speak to you, sir? I feel it is a matter of some importance." The Baron looked at the beautiful, golden girl in front of him and smiled.

"My dear, you sound so serious. What could make you this serious on such a beautiful evening?"

She felt her determination weaken before the hard, glittering gray eyes. His presence commanded her full attention. She lowered her attention from his compelling gaze and focused on his square, clean jaw and neatly trimmed moustache. She could feel him tensing, waiting. At her hesitation he studied her, studying the stylish gown which displayed her lovely, sloping shoulders.

She was about to speak when he licked his lower lip as his eyes strayed to her bosom. He reminded Marilyn of the old tomcat cook kept in her spotless New England kitchen. The old tom would lick his lips just that way when cook was setting about to pour him a saucer of cream. Only the tom's glittering green eyes would betray his excitement as he slowly and deliberately licked his whiskered chin. Marilyn knew the urbane exterior was a display he was making for her.

Marilyn plunged in. "I have heard rumors this day about the sickness of the Indians. Is this true? Is the Yellow Jack fever imminent?"

"My dear," the Baron said, concern on his face, "who has told you these tales? There are several Indians who appear to be ill, but mind you, I say *appear*," he said, wagging a finger in the air. "I am sure they are contemplating a rebellion of some sort. There have been vague threats that have reached my ears."

"But what of the living conditions? I have heard they are deplorable."

The Baron puffed out his cheeks in outrage. "Who tells you these tales? Answer me, my dear," he said coldly.

Marilyn stood her ground firmly. "I heard it at Mrs. Quince's plantation. The lady herself spoke of it."

"I will wager she got it from her neighbor to the north," the Baron said, his mouth tight.

So he already knew of the meeting with Sebastian at Mrs. Quince's. Evidently Carl had reported the details of the visit.

"Sebastian Rivera was there, yes. He no more than said hello and then good-bye. Mrs. Quince said that at one time the Yellow Jack was on this plantation and it spread to the others and many lives were lost."

The Baron snapped his fingers; the sound hung heavy in the still air. "One cannot concern oneself with the insignificance of the slaves."

Marilyn felt anger rise in her chest, but she fought to control it. She could not afford to lose her temper now. "Are you telling me, sir, that there is no fever here at Tree of Life?"

"But of course, my dear. That is exactly what I am telling you. There is no need for you to concern yourself with the running of the plantation. You and your father have for many years lived luxuriously and comfortably from the Tree of Life. Your father never once questioned my methods. The details are much too complex for you to even begin to understand."

"Sir, you are insinuating that I am not capable of handling my own affairs and that I would not understand them if I tried."

The Baron smiled coolly. "No, my dear. However, I feel that it is not something for you to concern yourself with. I will run this plantation the same as I have for all the years since I came here. Let this be the end of the discussion," he said abruptly.

Marilyn was still her father's daughter. "One moment, sir; there are several other things I wish to discuss." She trembled at the audacity she had shown. She squared her shoulders. "There is the matter of the children. I wish to know why they are not with their parents on the Regalo Verdad."

"The children remain here. They are part of a debt owed to me by their parents." His speech was smooth, but his cheek had begun to twitch. Marilyn knew he was angry. So be it. She, herself, could never remember being so angry.

"But sir, it is my understanding that Sebastian Rivera has offered to buy the girls for any amount of money you wanted."

"There is no need to discuss the matter, and my dear, I want you never to mention the name of Sebastian Rivera in Casa Grande again."

Marilyn felt herself flush. She looked at Jamie who was watching her. He appeared upset. He was rubbing his thumb and fingers together nervously. He was trying, for some reason, to catch his father's eye. The Baron ignored him and continued to stare at Marilyn.

"I repeat. The children are not for sale and never will be. Is that clear?" he asked in a dangerous voice.

Chagrin, humiliation, and defeat ran up Marilyn's spine. Again she looked at Jamie. He was now relaxed, his fingers still. Surely he did not enjoy her humiliation. She looked into the eyes of Carl and could only read pity. The Baron's eyes were cold and unreadable.

Refusing to give up, Marilyn ignored the flush that traversed her body and said brazenly, "I trust, sir, that I can depend on an accounting of my share of the plantation before the carnival begins."

There was a coldness in her quiet voice. She gathered up the bottom of the gown and advanced to the dining room at Elena's entrance to announce dinner. She did not wait for one of the men to escort her. She was mistress of this plantation and she would do as she pleased. She looked into the dark eyes of the housekeeper and could not fathom the look—admiration or hate. She carried herself regally and stood by the chair, waiting for Jamie to seat her.

Dinner was a dismal affair. The Baron had struck a note of fear within her, and the ominous phrases in her father's ledger swam before her eyes. Carl tried his best to make lively table conversation but his heart was not in it. Jamie spoke of the new order he had placed for five soldiers from England. They were to be made expressly for him and would arrive on the next sailing.

Marilyn picked at the food and answered when spoken to. She felt like a school girl who had been reprimanded.

The Baron chewed his food slowly and methodically and concentrated on the slim girl opposite him. What did this chit of a girl know? How dare she order him about! Actually order was too strong a word. It was all Sebastian Rivera's doing. He knew the man was behind all the questions and the innuendos.

The girl was probably smitten with Rivera, just as all the women in Brazil appeared to be. She was going to be trouble. He could feel it in his bones. If Carl did not take interest soon the plantation would suffer. As he chewed he contemplated the accounting the girl had requested. There was no way he could refuse. To do so would be illegal and make him look less a man. He looked at the girl coldly and was revolted by all she stood for. He hated her in that moment as much as he hated Sebastian Rivera. For a moment he was disconcerted and he momentarily lost the rhythm of his chewing. Marilyn looked up into the cold, hate-filled expression of the Baron and was shocked. She felt her body tremble and did not hear a question Jamie asked of her.

The Baron repeated the question for her benefit. For the life of her she did not know what he said. She nodded and asked to be excused, pleading a headache. The three men watched her exit, concern on their faces, concern for three different reasons.

As Marilyn passed the chair of the Baron she suppressed an urge to scream like Bartholomo had done: "The Baron is a nitwit; The Baron is a nitwit!" She raced on light feet to her room once she reached the hall. She passed the housekeeper in the hall and did not give her a second look. Once in her room she flung herself on the chaise and let the humiliation wash over her. Just because she was a woman the Baron thought she was incompetent.

A knock sounded on the door. Marilyn bade the caller to enter. It was Jamie, a frown on his face. "Does this mean you will not play the spinet this evening?" he asked wistfully.

"I fear not, Jamie. My head aches too much." In truth her head *had* begun to throb like a drum.

"Couldn't you take something to make it disappear? I have waited all day for this evening—just waited for you to play," he almost shouted, then immediately gained control of himself. "I am sorry," he said; "that was foolish of me. I so love music. Did you know we have an opera house? In Manaus."

Marilyn at the moment could not have cared less. She waited for him to leave. Evidently he had something else to say. She waited.

"Aren't you happy that the girls are to remain here to see to you?" He looked so concerned that she nodded. Anything so that he would leave. Marilyn closed her eyes in pain as he quietly left the room.

When the headache left her she would again get out the packet of her father's papers and read, and she would understand them if it took her till morning. Once the decision was made she dropped off into an uneasy sleep. The girls awoke her later in the evening and helped her dress for bed. She climbed between the crisp, cool sheets, her resolution postponed till the morrow.

Downstairs the Baron was having a heated discussion with Carl. "I want no more foolishness with the girl— Alicia. Did I not tell you to put her out of your mind? She is penniless. We don't need a pauper added to this family."

"But father, how do you cut love out of your heart?" Carl pleaded. The Baron looked at his son and his lip curled in distaste. He knew the boy would botch the job.

"You must do it. I am your father and I command you to obey me."

Carl nodded, his eyes wretched with the task before him. "The chit wants an accounting. Did you hear her? And what am I to do? I warn you, Carl, I give you till carnival. If you have not succeeded I will take other measures. And," he said ominously, "if you fail you will not marry Alicia. I will not have an impoverished lady of quality taking up room in my Casa Grande. Is that understood?"

Carl cringed before the verbal attack as though it had been physical. He knew what his father meant by "other measures."

Jamie sat on the sofa listening to the sharp words of his father. He wondered what had made the Baron so angry. Marilyn had agreed to everything he had said. He let his mind wander to the new order of the additional soldiers. It would bring his total to eighty. He did not hear Carl's weak reply promising to do his best.

The days stretched into weeks. Marilyn spent her days with Jamie and her evenings with Carl. At first she had spent many hours inspecting the Casa Grande. She picked the colorful tropical flowers and arranged them artfully in every room of the casa. She made her way to the kitchen regions and hesitantly made several suggestions to the cook. Surprisingly Elena made no attempt to interfere. When boredom set in, as Marilyn knew it would, she decided to teach Jamie the piano. He was not an apt pupil. He would have been content to have her play for him by the hour while he sat and dreamily listened. It puzzled Marilyn that his help was not needed on the plantation. The Baron actually seemed glad that he spent whole days in her company.

Carl was an attentive suitor. And he had fast become a suitor. On long, quiet evenings under the alluring tropical moon, Carl and Marilyn sat in the small pergola in the back gardens. He was pleasant company after the long days with Jamie. Carl, unlike his brother, was extremely well read and quite knowledgeable about the functions of rubber. He even described some ideas of his own for the practical use of the gooey substance drawn from trees.

Marilyn enjoyed these evenings with Carl. His excitement was contagious, and she found herself a sounding board for his more innovative ideas. She became quite fond of Carl; he was dear to her if only for the fact that he respected her intellect, acknowledged that she even possessed an intellect! A rare thing in an age where a woman was supposed blessed if she possessed tiny feet, slim ankles, a narrow waist, and a pretty face. Having these, a woman had no need for a brain. Indeed, society decried a woman who professed to have one.

Marilyn knew that several times Carl had been on the verge of asking for her hand. Skillfully she had so far avoided a direct confrontation. She was fond of Carl but she did not love him. His attentions were fast becoming worrisome to the golden-haired girl. She did not want to hurt him, yet he had to be told, so that he could pursue other interests. It was only fair to Carl.

She paid rapt attention to the lessons that Jamie and Carl taught her regarding the jungles, and the Baron finally decreed she could ride alone.

Marilyn arose early with the knowledge that this was her first day of freedom. For it was freedom! She could go and do as she pleased. In truth, all she planned to do was go for a ride alone, without Jamie or Carl. She was so excited she could barely close the hooks on her riding habit. She slipped quietly from the room, her carryall in her hand. She was going to the Gift of Truth, Sebastian Rivera's plantation. A note had been delivered from Mrs. Quince telling her of the expert needlewoman that Sebastian employed as his housekeeper. It appeared from the letter that Anna, for that was her name, had agreed not only to make Marilyn's costume but that of Mrs. Quince. Mrs. Quince herself was to be at the plantation awaiting Marilyn's arrival. She had journeyed there the day before and had spent the night.

Marilyn slipped from the house quietly and ran on light feet to the stable. Dawn was just breaking. She looked at the gray-pink light and shivered. By the time she had her horse saddled it would be completely light. She saddled the dappled gray with clumsy fingers. She fought the urge to look over her shoulder to see if anyone was coming to stop her. Her preparations completed, she mounted the gray and led him in a slow trot through the courtyard. Once on the jungle trail she spurred the horse gently and it responded to her hold on the reins. She felt as free as the colorful birds with their shrill raucous cries. She picked her way carefully over the vine-strewn ground; her seat was firm and she felt quite comfortable on her high perch. She nibbled on a ripe papaya, tossing the pit away. She rode at a fast canter and within the hour was on property that belonged to Sebastian Rivera.

Marilyn stopped her horse at the end of the long driveway and looked at the casa grande named Regalo Verdad. It had a personality of its own. Judging by its appearance, Marilyn felt that the people who lived there cared. There were no wandering chickens and no dirty, threadbare children running around. There were people on the grounds. True, they moved slowly, but that was indicative of the Indian. They were clean and smiling. Small children looked at her curiously as she slipped from the dappled gray and handed a tall, muscular Indian the reins. He offered a wide toothy smile. "Welcome Missy to Regalo Verdad." He gave a small formal bow to Marilyn's delight. She smiled in return. A small child took her by the hand and led her to the wide, ornate front door.

Marilyn looked at the small child. "Hello," she said smiling. "What is your name?"

"Mary. What is your name, miss?" she said in clear, precise English.

"Marilyn Bannon. You may call me Marilyn if you like." The child smiled shyly.

"You are very pretty," she said, her dark eyes lighting up.

"And I think you are very pretty, too. I love pigtails on little girls," Marilyn said, twitching the fat pigtail.

"What is pigtail?" the child asked.

Marilyn laughed in delight. She held the heavy braid and explained that it was called a pigtail in the United States. The child giggled over the new word. Marilyn watched as she rolled the word over and over on her tongue. The door was opened by the housekeeper. She ushered Marilyn into a wide, cool-looking room and immediately Marilyn spied Mrs. Quince drinking a cup of coffee, her host next to her.

Once again Marilyn was struck by Sebastian's resemblance to the Baron. The same square jaw, the set of the eyes. Consciously she drew her eyes away from his face.

As she entered he arose and extended a warm welcome to his casa grande, but his eyes remained cool and aloof. Immediately he excused himself and left the ladies to their dressmaking. He informed his housekeeper that he would be back in time for lunch, and if she had time, to prepare it. The dark-skinned housekeeper smiled and said, "Be gone with you, Sebastian. When you return, it will be ready. As you well know, I am quite capable of doing two things at one time." Sebastian smiled and his handsome face transformed completely. Marilyn envied the easy camaraderie he had with his housekeeper. Why couldn't he smile at *her* like that?

The ladies then entered into an animated discussion about the carnival costumes they would wear.

"What will you be wearing for the carnival, Mrs. Quince? Or are you keeping it a secret?"

"No secret, Marilyn. I don't wear a costume. I'm far too old for that. I'll just go as plain old me."

Marilyn laughed softly. "Don't consider yourself old, Mrs. Quince. You're ageless! And as for being plain, nothing could be farther from the truth."

"She is right, Mrs. Quince," Anna broke in. "There is a character about you, a queenly aura. Are you not the most respected lady in Manaus?" Then, turning to Marilyn, "I feel Mrs. Quince has no need of a costume. However, such is not the case for you. Have you decided what it will be? With your height and bearing you remind me of a goddess. Marilyn, what would you say to the idea of appearing as Diana—the huntress?"

Marilyn was speechless.

"Good, it's settled then," Mrs. Quince burst out. "Diana you shall be."

Anna, the housekeeper, watched the golden girl and said, "I shall outdo myself in making your costume. It will be a small payment for the kindness you have shown my daughter."

It was then Mrs. Quince explained that Anna was Nessie's mother.

Noontime arrived and Anna departed for the kitchen. Mrs. Quince looked at Marilyn. "Tell me, child. What do you think of Regalo Verdad? In Portuguese it means "The Gift of Truth.""

"It's magnificent," Marilyn said honestly.

"Sebastian's heart and soul are in this plantation. I think he has worked harder than any man in Brazil."

Later, Anna announced lunch and the two women followed her to the dining room where they were immediately joined by Sebastian. He seated the two women and then took his place at the head of the table. He bowed his head and said grace. The light luncheon of fresh fish was a tasty delight. For dessert there was a fresh pineapple and guava salad. The inevitable strong Brazilian coffee followed.

Mrs. Quince, a matchmaker at heart, suddenly spoke. "Sebastian, my dear, why do you not take Marilyn for a ride around the plantation? Anna has finished with her for the moment. She will only be in the way here."

Marilyn flushed a rosy crimson at the blatant approach of her matchmaking. Sebastian Rivera frowned, but being the gentleman he was, agreed. He told Marilyn to wait on the veranda and he would have her mount saddled. He returned within minutes. Marilyn looked up at the tall man. "I apologize for Mrs. Quince. I am sure you must have other things to occupy your time and taking me riding is not one of them. Perhaps we can let it go till some other time. I can sit on the veranda if Mrs. Quince feels that I am in the way."

Sebastian looked at the golden girl and felt some of his reserve fade. "It is my pleasure, Miss Bannon," he said gallantly. He helped Marilyn mount and her dappled gray followed the black horse.

"It is a magnificent animal you ride, sir," she said in a friendly tone. Sebastian merely nodded.

"I shall take you to see the quarters of my workers. I would also like you to see the other parents of the little girls that are in service at the 'Tree,' " he said coldly.

They rode in silence and soon came upon what looked like a village. The stone huts were whitewashed and clean. Small children scampered around happy and healthy. The women wore bright clothing; they too looked happy and healthy. The jungle had been cleared from the center of the little village. Everything seemed to have its place. The people greeted Sebastian happily; smiles stretched from ear to ear. It seemed that Sebastian had a personal word for each. And he appeared to know everyone's name. He reached a long arm down and scooped up a small Indian boy and swung him onto the horse. He spurred the great black beast around the small clearing and the child giggled and laughed with glee. His mother smiled at this display of affection from the owner of the plantation. Marilyn felt in awe of this great man at her side, yet he mystified her. Suddenly he set the child down and called out in the Indian tongue. Three women came to stand by his mount and looked at him expectantly. Sebastian introduced Marilyn and told them she lived on the Tree of Life and that she knew the children.

Hope, despair, and love were mirrored in the women's faces, but they said nothing. They stood still and waited for her to speak. She tried but the words were thick in her throat. She tried again. "Dear God in heaven, what do I say?" She looked at Sebastian. He returned her look mockingly. She would receive no help from him. She cleared her throat. "Help me, dear God," she pleaded. She looked into the still faces of the women

in front of her. Suddenly the little village was quiet.
They all waited for her answer. "The girls are happy.
Father John is teaching them their letters and numbers.
Moriah is happy and laughs a lot. One of the women,
evidently Moriah's mother, beamed a smile, tears in her
eyes. The others asked of Rosy and Bridget. Marilyn tried
to speak quickly, but her feeling caused her to stutter.
Sebastian did not fail to notice her emotion but he said
nothing—if the girl was to live with the Newsomes then
she was just as responsible as they.

The flat dark face of Moriah's mother looked at Marilyn and her eyes pleaded and the tears escaped the
bright, golden eyes and flowed down her cheeks.

Marilyn looked at the three mothers and cleared her
throat.

Finally she managed, "They will be returned to you by
the end of the carnival. I give you my word." Suddenly
the women were grasping at her legs and crying happily.
Marilyn looked at Sebastian but could not read anything
in his look. "I will see to it that the children are returned," she said coldly to the tall man. "I do not give
my word lightly, sir."

"It is not your word that I doubt, Miss Bannon. It is
that of Carlyle Newsome. And," he said darkly, "*he* has
given *his* word that the children will not be returned—
ever!"

"Well, Sebastian Rivera," Marilyn said hotly, "I have
given you my word. And," she said imperiously, "that is
the end of that." She reined in the gray and started off
at a brisk canter. Sebastian caught up to her effortlessly.
There was a new look on his face. He studied the proud
head and the stately carriage of the golden girl. She had
spirit and determination. Perhaps he had been mistaken.
He shook his head. Had he not just heard in town but
three days ago that she was to marry Carl Newsome?

"Tell me, Miss Bannon, when do you plan to marry
Carl?"

"I am afraid you have been misinformed, sir. I am
not now or in the future contemplating marriage with
Carl. That, sir, was an erroneous rumor you heard.

Somehow I would have thought you were not the type of man to listen to gossip," she said, her voice frigid, her face hot.

Sebastian looked at the girl and did not doubt her for one moment.

"And to clarify one more matter, Mr. Rivera—" she made his name sound like a disease—"when I marry it will be because I am in love with my whole heart. I will have no marriage arranged for me for convenience's sake. Is that understood? The man I marry must be a man, and above all else, he must love me as I love him, the man who is to be the father of my children." Marilyn flushed from head to toe. Dear God! Had she said these things aloud? So be it. She was her father's daughter; she would speak her mind. This was a time when one could speak as one chose. She had certainly done that, she smiled to herself. Mrs. Quince would be delighted when she heard.

Marilyn spurred her horse forward, leaving a startled Sebastian staring after her.

Sebastian watched her ride ahead, a smile on his face. She *was* a spitfire! Perhaps she would survive in this tortuous land after all.

Suddenly Sebastian saw a long vine hanging in the path of the unseeing Marilyn. She was heading for it at a fast pace, unaware of the danger. He dug his heels into the horse's flanks, spurring the beast forward. Lunging to Marilyn's side, he reached for her and grabbed her from the saddle just as the horse cleared the vine.

Marilyn found herself in a most unladylike position. In order to extricate herself, she would either have to wiggle out of his grasp and fall to the ground, placing her in an embarrassing position, or she would have to let Sebastian pull her up next to him, placing her face inches from his dark brown face. Sebastian looked at her curiously, waiting to see the decision she would make. She nodded slightly, and he pulled her up to him.

Sebastian's eyes laughed into Marilyn's. The jet circles glinted in amusement at her obvious predicament. Brazenly, her own eyes stared back into his.

He felt the amusement die in him as he became conscious of her nearness. Her womanly scent mingled with the perfume of her hair. The bright Brazilian sun made a nimbus of gold about her head. He held her more tightly and found himself marveling at the lightness of her body and the slimness of her waist. The contact of her body against his thigh was warm, a tingle of slow-burning fire. He stared deeply into her eyes, and saw golden flecks dancing there, heightening the pink flush of her smooth cheek. He found himself bending his head lower, lower, until he could see a slight pulse at the base of her throat. Next thing he knew, he was kissing her, this golden goddess, and she was returning his kiss, in a way he thought no American girl knew how to kiss. Deeply, searchingly, passionately!

His lips were warm, soft, demanding. She felt her body respond to the surging passion which overcame her. She had never experienced a feeling such as this. She wanted the lovely warmth to stay with her forever.

Sebastian broke away first. He apologized profusely. His face was unreadable. Marilyn's face was a mask of confusion. She did not understand. Did he not enjoy it as much as she did? She looked into his face again and still could read nothing.

She flushed with shame. Evidently he was used to kissing women; it meant nothing to him! If he kept a woman in residence in Para, as Jamie had whispered to her in confidence, he certainly did not need her! Shame made her tongue sharp.

"Please put me down!" she said coldly. It was Sebastain's turn to be perplexed. Women! he thought in disgust. They were all alike! One moment you think you know what they want and the next they do or say the opposite. He could have sworn she liked the kiss; the decision had been hers to make!

Marilyn mounted the gray and headed back to the plantation. Coming into the courtyard she slid down from her mount and raced into the house. Mrs. Quince and the housekeeper looked at her in dismay. Shyness not being one of Mrs. Quince's better virtues, that good lady wailed, "What happened, child?"

Marilyn plopped herself down in a very unladylike manner and stared ahead stonily, her face a mask of indignation.

Sebastian strode into the room. He looked at the three women and cringed before the attack of the housekeeper.

"What did you do? What did you do to this beautiful girl? Can you not see she is a lady? Why is she so upset? Tell me, you big oaf," she shrilled, "what did you do?"

Sebastian suffered the verbal abuse of his housekeeper, much as he would have were she his mother. Mrs. Quince took up the cry.

"Lord a mercy, Sebastian, what is it? She says nothing; she just stares!"

Sebastian stood first on one foot and then the other, twirling his hat in his hands, much like a child. "I only kissed her," he said defensively.

"Ahh!" said the housekeeper, smiling.

"Lord a mercy!" exclaimed Mrs. Quince.

Sebastian basked in the approval of the two ladies.

Marilyn stood up and looked at the smiling Sebastian. He could smile now that the two older ladies appeared to be on his side. "Don't ever kiss me again!" she said haughtily. "When I want to be kissed, I shall ask to be kissed."

The tears welled in her eyes and again flowed down her cheeks.

Sebastian glanced at the three women. Now they all held cold looks. He had made the golden girl cry!

He stomped from the room muttering something about vaporous women. He would go to Manaus and his sloe-eyed beauty. She at least would not have the vapors.

# 7

Carl rode beside his father into the lower acreage of the plantation. They rode in silence, each concentrating on his own thoughts. Carl was thinking, as usual, of the lovely Alicia. Why did this golden-haired young woman have to come from America and place him in this predicament? Why could she have not stayed where she belonged and leave him to convince his father of the merits of having a well-bred wife to enhance the halls of the "Tree" casa. Now, with Marilyn actually here, there was little hope of doing so. His luck had run amuck and when she arrived it was evident that she was beautiful. This was another reason why he could not go against his father's wishes; he could not say that he could not consummate a marriage with her. If she had been ugly, it would have been easier, since his father himself was a lover of beautiful women. Alicia, Alicia—why did your father work himself into so unsavory a position and then quit this world, leaving you and your mother to suffer the consequences of his folly, dear Alicia?

The Baron stole a glance at his elder son and curled his lip in distaste. He supposed the fool was mooning over that little mouse, Alicia. What he saw in her was a mystery. It disappointed him to have his son have so little regard for the "Tree" and wish to install an impoverished waif as mistress of the casa. Why couldn't the fool see it was almost as easy to emerge from the marriage ceremony having benefited moneywise as well as by having a lovely woman to grace his bed—a woman such as Marilyn. He felt a warmth in his loins as he thought of her. Little snit though he thought her, he was, nevertheless, greatly attracted to her. She was the loveliest woman he had seen in Brazil since Elena was a young girl. Elena, once so beautiful and sweet, now so rigid and cold. It had been many years since he had crept into her bed in the dark hours of the night to enjoy her warm arms and feel her young body bending to his. When had she turned against him? It seemed it was soon after his wife's death. He shrugged in confusion. Women, he supposed, were always to be the enigma of man. But Marilyn—Marilyn would be worth the effort to please. She would be a prize, that one. How he wished he were a young man again. He would not waste one moment to persuade her to be mistress of the "Tree" and mistress of his passions. If only Jamie were able to . . .

"Father," Carl said in a quiet voice, "I know you don't wish to speak of this, but it is of great importance to me, and for once, I wish you to hear me out."

"I thought you were riding along mooning over that little mouse. I've told you before, I do not wish to speak of her. That is a closed book! You have your duty to the "Tree" and I will not have you shirk it. Do you understand, Carl? All else in life is unimportant. The "Tree" is your life. I will have it no other way!"

"Father, for once you will hear me out. There are no servants here to listen to our conversation and there is no house guest to upset and disturb. You will hear what I have to say."

Seeing himself at a disadvantage, the Baron nodded his head and gazed straight ahead as his horse plodded onward. He gave his consent, allowing Carl to speak for the last time of Alicia.

"Father, I love Alicia. I feel I cannot live without her. I need her, father. Her state of finances is not her doing. It was her father who was foolhardy. You must give me my head and let me marry her. I love her, father." His last words came out as sobs. He immediately stifled them, knowing how his father detested unmanly emotions.

"Her father was a twit and she would bear you twits for sons. In my business dealings with the old fellow, I had first-hand knowledge of his foolishness and lack of business sense. How do you suppose we were able to send the last six dividends to Marilyn's father so that he would not know we were having difficulties with the 'Tree'?"

The Baron's last word settled into Carl's brain with the weight of a lead boot. "You! You were the cause of her father losing his holdings! Dear Alicia said he had been cheated, but being a lady and loving me, she never once said it was you who cheated the old gentleman. You have ruined a fine old family, and you wish to further yourself by denying the old man's daughter a chance at a new life. How could you be so cruel? Have you no heart? Can't you understand I love her?"

"I have no use for your petty emotions. There is nothing that means more to me than the 'Tree.' When my own father disinherited me it was for a far lesser offense than denying loyalty to the 'Tree.' It was only when he died leaving no other heir that I was able to come back from England and take up my rightful place here in the plantation. Be careful, Carl. If you go against my orders, you will no longer be my son! You will leave the 'Tree' and all it stands for and forage for yourself in the jungles. Mind my words! I will not hear of this subject again. You must make your choice and stand by it!"

The Baron watched the shocked look on Carl's face and knew he had won. The young fool was not about to see himself disinherited. No, he was too fond of the leisurely life and the accoutrements of wealth. The young fop knew his ground and knew he had lost. The Baron looked at his pocket watch, and smiled inwardly as he thought of the little coup taking place at this very moment on Regalo Verdad. He spurred his horse forward so Carl would not see the smile that spread over his face.

Sebastian peeked into the room and saw Anna clearing away the tea tray. "Have Mrs. Quince and Miss Bannon left, Anna?"

"Yes sir. They left a few moments ago. Where have you been hiding?"

"Don't be insolent." He smiled at her. "I have only been out to the gardens to see what progress is being made in cutting the jungle back to its proper confines. You say they left? I didn't hear them ride out or I would have said my good-byes to them."

"I do not think Miss Bannon missed your presence, Sebastian. In fact, I am sure she was greatly relieved when you did not appear."

"Yes," he said coldly, remembering Marilyn's rebuff. "I am sure she was. Nevertheless, I would have liked to have said my good-bye to Mrs. Quince and wish her to give her husband my sincere regrets that he was unable to join us this afternoon. I, too, should have seen to my duties instead of playing host to women's tea.

"Fetch me a glass of sherry, Anna. I will have it on the veranda," he said as he moved toward the open doors to sit on the white rattan chairs gracing the wide portico.

He was sipping on the sherry and reading one of his textbooks when Jesus, the plantation foreman, came running up to the house.

"Mr. Rivera, come quickly. There is trouble!"

"What trouble, Jesus?" Sebastian's voice mirrored the excitement in his foreman's voice.

"On the upper lots, where we have just installed the new curing houses. There is a fire. We had it just about under control when I left to get you. Mr. Rivera, most of the new sap has been spilled and wasted or burned. There is little we can do to salvage it, I'm afraid. Come, perhaps you will know what we can do."

"A fire? How? Those smoke pots for curing have been checked. I have seen to every precaution. Someone has been careless. Who was it?"

Sebastian watched fear creep into the foreman's face. The man hesitated before he spoke again. "No, Mr. Rivera; it was not due to carelessness. Someone deliberately set that fire. One of the men found the kerosene-soaked rags."

"Deliberately? How can that be? Where were the men tending the smoke pots?"

"They were beaten and tied. No one saw who the men were. They wore hoods."

"Say no more, Jesus. I have a very good idea who they were, or least who they were hired by. But I have no proof."

"It is so fortunate the bulk of the rubber was not at the curing house. Were it not for the lead wagon losing a wheel, and holding up the rest for more than two hours, very nearly all the rubber we have harvested in the past three months would have been lost in the fire."

"Yes, Jesus. It is most fortunate. We will cure the sap at the old curing house and still be in time for the shipment to Para. If we lose any more time, the streams will be dried up by the time our shipment is ready. Come, let us go see what damage has been done."

# 8

Marilyn sat in her room at the "Tree," contemplating her next move with the Baron. Exasperated because her efforts to have the children rejoin their parents at Regalo Verdad had been thwarted, she was determined to find something with which to bargain, something which would sway the Baron's thinking.

Opening the valise which contained her father's papers, she examined them, searching for the title rights to the "Tree." There were phrases she hadn't understood when she had looked at them last, and she had decided to bring them to Father John in the hopes that he could shed some light on them. It wouldn't be to her benefit to ask the Baron or to inquire of the Baron's lawyer.

They would just put her off and tell her not to busy her pretty little head about it. No, Father John would be the best one to answer her questions.

Placing the papers back in the valise, her hand brushed against a hardbound book—her father's ledger.

Pushing aside the flood of renewed grief, she opened the ledger to those puzzling pages. Instantly, she thought of Mr. Quinton, the lawyer who had written to her father and informed him of . . . what? What exactly did Mr. Quinton tell her father that induced him to repudiate the Baron. Surely, it was not only because Princess Isabel's *Ventre Livre* law was being ignored. No, there were hints of something which Richard Bannon could not forgive. Was it killing slaves? Yes, that too. But there was something more; she was sure of it. Her eyes glanced over the words, "cruelly beating the slave till his death."

Marilyn felt cold waves race up her spine. Behind those glinting, steel gray eyes was a killer.

Carefully she put the ledger back and laid the valise on the floor of the clothespress. She intended to go to the kitchen and speak to Elena. Perhaps the housekeeper would be able to tell her where she could find this Mr. Quinton.

The kitchen was dim and cool, shuttered from the heat of the day. Elena was there, instructing the Indian cook and sorting through the pantries making a shopping list. At the arrival of Marilyn, she lifted her dark head and faced the intruder with cold, hostile eyes.

"Elena, I wish to speak with you a moment, if you have the time. I'd like to ask you a few questions, if I may." Why was she acting so meek? Angry with herself, she said in a more authoritative tone, "Now, Elena!"

Elena set aside her pen and approached the waiting Marilyn in a most respectful manner. Marilyn modulated her voice, slightly apologetic for the harsh tone she had used.

"Yes, Miss Bannon, may I be of any assistance?"

"As a matter of fact, Elena, you may. I have remembered my father speaking of an old acquaintance, a Mr.

Quinton. I was wondering if perhaps you might know where I can find him. I happen to know he was a lawyer and he has since retired."

"I may be able to help you, Miss Bannon," said Elena, her black eyes glinting with unspoken curiosity. It gave Marilyn some satisfaction to know that Elena's facade of seeming indifference could be pierced.

"Mr. Quinton was once barrister to the Newsome family, when the old Baron was alive. He was a frequent visitor to the 'Tree' when the Baron held residence in the old Casa Grande. Since the death of the old Baron and the burning of the original casa, I've not seen him. Indeed, it has been years since I've heard his name mentioned in this house. The Baron does not welcome Mr. Quinton here; he had a falling out with the gentleman soon after the death of the old Baron. I assure you, Miss Bannon, the Baron would not take kindly to the idea of your seeking Mr. Quinton out." At this last, Elena's voice grew cold with warning.

"I don't care if the Baron takes kindly to the idea or not. He has no jurisdiction over whom I may or may not see. Now answer my question, Elena; do you know where I can find Mr. Quinton?"

Elena's eyes were guarded and she lowered her voice to a degree above a whisper. "You will find Mr. Quinton at his townhouse in Manaus. Crampton Avenue, I believe. It is the large house with stone lions at the foot of the drive."

"Thank you, Elena. Now if you will tell the groom to saddle my horse, I'll be going for my ride today, as usual."

Marilyn spurred the horse forward. It was time to look at the living quarters of her Indians and blacks. Sebastian had not said the words aloud. Still she knew what he meant. Go look and compare. See what you are living off. Well, she would see, and she would see now. She let her mind wander to the day of the ride and how she had found herself in Sebastian's arms. She could feel herself flush. She knew the heat had nothing to do with the flush that spread over her body. She was so engrossed in her thoughts that she did not notice Jamie until he rode in front of her and startled her. Quickly he reined in his mount and laughed. "I will give you a penny if you tell me what you were thinking," he teased.

Marilyn smiled. "Just about my costume for the ball." Jamie's face lit up at the mention of the ball and costumes. "What will you wear, Marilyn?" he coaxed.

Marilyn wagged a finger. "You shall have to wait and see, Jamie Newsome," she teased back. "What will you wear?"

Jamie smiled secretively, "I shall not tell you. I want you to be surprised when you see me. Tell me, where are you riding to this morning?"

"I plan to look over the Indians' village. Would you like to accompany me?"

Jamie looked shocked. "Does my father know what you are doing?" he asked nervously.

"No, Jamie. I did not think I would have to ask permission to look over land half of which is mine," she said, her tone bitter.

Jamie looked at her and did not know what to say.

"It is not far now, just around the—" As they approached the small village, Marilyn could hear voices. She strained higher on her mount to see into the clearing. As they rode nearer, she could not at first believe her eyes. Never in her whole life had she seen such squalor. At the sound of the horses' hooves the noise abated. Children as well as the men and the women stood quietly; they wore rags, their faces covered with sores. The children had bowed legs, a sure sign of rickets. They looked at the two on horseback with sneers on their faces. The open hostility was so obvious that Marilyn wondered how Jamie could sit so still on his horse and say nothing. The hostility was for him. Of this she was sure. The men had blank, hopeless looks on their faces. The women stood mute as their children whined in hunger. Marilyn felt physically sick. She let her eyes wander around the village. The sanitary conditions were so bad that the stench made her eyes water.

God in heaven! She gave her mount a gentle prod and continued around the small village holding her breath all the while. The blacks were separated from the Indians, but they looked in much the same condition. The only difference was that they looked ill, physically very ill. A mound of dirt behind the squalid huts caught her eye. She knew immediately what it was. A grave! As her eyes continued to wander she noticed two more fresh mounds. A tall black walked into the middle of the clearing. Marilyn closed her eyes in shock as the whip marks and welts on the man's back glistened in the bright sun. Marilyn fought down a retch as she demanded to know how many people were sick. No one answered her. "Jamie," she called. "Come here. Ask them how many are sick. Immediately!"

Jamie looked angry for the moment but obeyed her command. "A dozen or so," he replied shortly.

"What is being done?" she demanded.

Again Jamie spoke. "The veterinarian was here," he said shortly.

"You mean the animal doctor?" Marilyn said, outraged.

Jamie nodded. "He said they are just lazy, that they are not sick," he said happily.

"Not sick! They all look sick to me," she said again, the anger showing in her voice.

Again she spurred her horse forward to observe. In the far corner of the clearing she noticed a penlike enclosure. She rode over to it and looked at the dozen or so small children sitting on the ground playing in the dirt.

"Why are they in this pen?" she demanded of Jamie.

"We are breeding them. They are the best. They get the best food and the best clothing. They are the pick of the litter," Jamie giggled.

"They're nothing but babies," Marilyn wailed in agony. "Just babies." She looked again at the women standing quietly about. Hate and fear rode rampant across their faces. Hatred she could understand, but not the fear. Why of her and Jamie? Surely they did not fear that she would take their babies from them, too? She had never in her wildest imagination seen such misery and human suffering. They were human beings without a glimmer of hope and there was nothing but hard labor and squalor for them on their horizons. She thought of Sebastian and his village. The difference was like night and day. She wondered if he knew what this village looked like. She prayed he did not. She wanted no one to know that she was responsible for half of this.

"Why are you so angry, Marilyn?" Jamie pleaded.

Marilyn was speechless. "Do you not think I have a right to be angry, Jamie?"

"Why, Marilyn?" Jamie said, snapping his fingers. "They are just slaves."

"Don't ever snap your fingers at me again, Jamie. Do you hear me? Not ever," Marilyn shrilled as she spurred her horse from the clearing. "Not ever again!" she shouted.

Jamie rode behind the now silent Marilyn. He knew she was angry, just as Elena was angry sometimes. He did not understand the reason. He had only done what his father did. Why should that make her angry?

Marilyn ached with a physical as well as a mental sickness as she pondered the problem. She was disgusted when she thought of all the fine things she had in life and that all the advantages were bought with the sweat and the deaths of these downtrodden people. She took solace in the thought that her dear father did not know where his fortune had come from. She was sure that if he had known he would have made complete revisions. Her heart heavy, she thought how like her father she was. If he would have done something then so would she. At the moment she was helpless. She could not ruin the carnival festivities for everyone. But the moment it came to an end she would take matters into her own hands. If she could not succeed then she would persuade Mrs. Quince and her husband to help her. She could never live with this on her conscience. If necessary she would approach Sebastian Rivera. And the Baron! Well, she still had the accounting due her!

Jamie led the silent, sweating horses to the stable. Marilyn climbed wearily up the veranda and fell into the rattan chair. Within minutes of closing her eyes, she was sound asleep. She didn't know how long she had been asleep when the sound of voices awoke her. She was momentarily confused as she listened to the voices from indoors. It appeared that Jamie and Elena were arguing over something. She knew she should get up and leave so she wouldn't appear to be eavesdropping, but the heat stifled her and she sat mute. She didn't have the energy to move and go to her room. She would pretend she did not hear the voices and just blot them out of her hearing. She could not succeed at this, however. Jamie's high-pitched whine could not be ignored.

"They say they are too busy to play, Elena," he complained. "Father and Carl are too busy and you do not have the time. Marilyn is angry about the Indians at the village and she does not want to talk to me. What am I to do? The girls all said they had many things to do. I'm lonely."

"Jamie," came the tender reply, "why don't you get your soldiers and set them up on the veranda. Soon it will be cooler and I will bring you a drink."

"I don't want to get out the soldiers and I don't want a cool drink. I want someone to play with me."

"The servants are all busy. They have many chores to do, Jamie. You must understand that this is a very busy plantation and the work load is heavy. Everyone has to do his share. Besides, boys should play with boys."

"There are no boys to play with," Jamie sighed, logically. "Moriah is so pretty and she feels so soft."

Elena felt a chill ripple over her body. "Have you touched her? Jamie, answer me. Have you touched Moriah?"

"I just pinch her arm," Jamie pouted.

"Jamie, how many times have I told you? How many times have I warned you that Indian fathers get angry when you want to 'play' with their little girls."

"Stupid old Indians. No one cares and no one sees me 'play.' " A loud crash followed the petulant outburst.

Marilyn sat quietly, her mind racing at this strange talk from Jamie and Elena. It sounded like Jamie was feeble-minded. Her heart chilled at the horrible thought. It couldn't be. Not Jamie. *Yes, Jamie,* her mind answered her. Suddenly she began to recall the times she had seen Jamie playfully tug at Moriah's fat braids or the hair of one of the other girls. She also remembered the look of fright on the girls' faces at his seeming playfulness. She had thought it because he was the Baron's son, and that they were afraid to offend him. Now—she shuddered —she knew differently.

Suddenly she could hear running feet; Jamie ran down the steps and did not heed the heart-rending cry from Elena. "Jamie, come back. Come back, Jamie." Marilyn sat quietly and did not move. She did not want to intrude into a family matter. Now she was beginning to understand many things as she listened to Elena sob heartbrokenly from inside the casa.

Elena slumped into the hard wooden chair and wept as she hadn't wept in years. Poor Jamie. Had she been too hard on the boy? No, he had to learn and if he didn't, there would be grave trouble for him. They might even take him away. She sobbed anew as she thought of her life without Jamie. He was all she lived for. Life without him would be unendurable. How strange, she thought. Now I love him as if he were my own, but there was the day I hated the fat, pink-skinned baby. She thought of the Baron and the Baron's dead wife. The Baron had taken Elena as his mistress. He had lied to her and told her he no longer slept with his English wife. Then the English wife had become heavy with child, and Elena was given the job of handmaiden to Lady Newsome. Elena remembered the birth of Jamie and the one day in particular that Lady Newsome and the Baron had gone off in the carriage to some event on a neighboring plantation. Jamie had been left in her care. Angry with the circumstances she had been placed in, Elena had left the baby unattended and when she returned he had fallen and lay unconscious. He had remained in that unconscious state for four days. She also remembered the day the Baron had told her she must go and get rid of the baby she carried within her. He did not want any bastards in this house. She had done away with her own child and then had been expected to care for this white-skinned brat.

Soon it was evident to the most casual observer that Jamie did not function as well as Carl had at the same age. He appeared slow at first. While his body grew to manhood, his mind stayed as that of a child. She remembered when the Baron's wife finally accepted the fact that Jamie was feeble-minded; she took to her bed and just pined away for the child. Within a year Lady Newsome was dead and Elena's hatred of the Baron increased day by day. Guilty over her negligence of the child, she had appointed herself the child's guardian. She had come to love the child, Jamie, as much as she would have loved the child she at one time had carried within her.

She recalled how proud and in love she had been with the arrogant Baron when he had taken her for his mistress. She cringed as she remembered the lying words of love he had professed for her.

Now this. Jamie's preoccupation with the little Indian girls. I hope Miss Bannon has her way and the children are sent back to their parents. How much better it would be for all concerned. Especially for Jamie. Then there would be nothing to tempt him. Elena had told the Baron of Jamie's appetite and the Baron's answer had been a coarse laugh. "Why, Elena, you surprise me. What a delicate choice of words! And tell me," he whispered as he clutched her elbow, squeezing it painfully, "why do you feel you must be delicate with me? Have we not known moments when delicacy was abandoned for something more basic and infinitely more exciting?" His hard gray eyes peered into hers meaningfully, and Elena could feel the slow, hot, painful flush of color come to her face. "And as for Jamie," the baron continued, apparently enjoying Elena's embarrassment, "why else should one amass a fortune, if not to bring to one's son those things which he desires?" Elena pulled away from his grasp and quickly took her leave. Behind her she could hear the Baron's cruel laughter.

# 9

Sebastian took the steps to this townhouse two at a time. He was eager to see Aloni after all these weeks. The hassle at the dock had not done his humor any benefit, and he knew Aloni would be able to soothe his ruffled temper.

As he thrust the door open she came running to greet him. Her small, lithe figure was in his arms and she was kissing him, murmuring soft endearments.

"Come," she said, detaching herself from his arms, "I will prepare you a cool drink."

"It's not a drink I want, Aloni," he whispered hoarsely, pulling her back to him.

Aloni giggled seductively. "Oh, my strong, handsome master; tell Aloni what it is you want. Tell me, Sebastian." she cooed enticingly.

"You little tease," he answered huskily as a familiar surging coursed through his body.

Playfully, she struggled away from him and skipped up the first few steps to the bedroom. Sebastian bounded up the steps in hot pursuit, laughing uproariously at her little game. Her ritual never failed to amuse him.

He followed her to the top of the stairs and watched article after article being thrown through the open doorway, in accompaniment to her squeals of expectation.

First her tiny slippers and then her petticoats; faster and faster the clothing flew through the air. He dodged a

high-flying chemise and began to wonder at her agility
in undressing herself so quickly.

When the assault of clothing ended, he strode into the
dimly lit bedroom, cool from the shutters being drawn
against the afternoon sun. His eyes adjusted to the half-
light and found her lying atop the bed, waiting for him.
Sebastian stood before her, appraisingly, as he began to
remove his shirt. Through slitted eyes, their gaze locked.
His hands fumbled with his straining trousers as he saw
her. The pink tip of her tongue moistened her lips. As
always he was struck with her beauty. Her lean, supple
body never failed to excite him; her sensuous lips promised fulfillment; her sleek eyes measured him knowingly,
unashamedly. Aloni realized the impact her beauty had on
him and she capitalized on it.

He stood throbbing before her, enjoying the sight of
her breasts with their chocolate-colored nipples. Aloni
lowered her eyes and held her arms out for him.

Sebastian stood in front of his shaving stand. He
averted his eyes from the reflection which bore a startling resemblance to his enemy, the Baron. He noticed
Aloni's image in his shaving mirror. Her eyes were troubled as she studied him. He steeled himself against her
onslaught of questions. He had heard them so often. "Is
not Aloni pretty enough? Why can't I go with you? Are
you ashamed of your Aloni?" And on and on she would
whine, until he was dressed and ready to leave without
her. Then it was as though she were afraid he would order her from his house and she would change tactics and
once again become his sweet, undemanding Aloni.

"I think maybe Aloni will be leaving." A sob caught
in her throat.

Sebastian turned to face her, startled at her words.

She saw the questioning look he shot her. "It is true. I
think maybe Aloni will have to leave. My Sebastian has
thoughts for another."

"What are you saying, Aloni? I have no thoughts for
another." Even as he said the words, he knew he lied. It
was true; their lovemaking was clouded by his thoughts

of Marilyn. At one point he had almost uttered her name.

"This is true. Sebastian has found another. Is it one of those milk-skinned, overfed ladies you see at the opera house? No, Sebastian would not care for a fat lady. Perhaps," she said shrewdly, "it is the golden girl I have heard them speak of in the market place."

He denied the accusation hotly and said he wished to hear no more. "It is," she said whiningly. "It is the golden girl!"

Angry at the insight of his mistress, he snatched up his jacket and strode from the room.

She followed after him, small sobs catching in her throat. Anger welled up in him and he felt the urge to slap her, to still the words that tumbled from her lovely mouth. Immediately he was contrite and ashamed of the impulse. What's gotten into me? Have I gone mad? Within him beat the answer—Marilyn Bannon.

"I have business, Aloni. I'll be back this evening. Have something light for dinner. Perhaps we can go to the Chancor Gardens tonight and dance. Would you like that?"

He knew Aloni would like it. She was always begging him to take her out. "Aloni has no need for these pretty gowns. Aloni never goes anywhere where she can be seen," she would pout.

He watched her face light up. She came to him and threw her arms around his neck and kissed him gratefully. "You make Aloni so happy!"

"Yes," he answered curtly. "Be ready when I get back."

He strode over to his waiting coach and instructed the driver, "Crampton Avenue. We're going to Mr. Quinton's."

Sebastian settled back in the comfortable coach as it made its way through the traffic to Crampton Avenue.

Damn. He was annoyed. When would Aloni grow up? It grated on his nerves to hear her use her name instead of the personal pronoun. On reflection, he noticed that he was becoming bored with her. Since his return from

the East. Just after his meeting Marilyn Bannon. *Damn,*
he swore silently. *That golden-haired she-devil has a
way of getting under my skin!* Settling back further in
his seat, he pushed his thoughts away from Marilyn and
toward the afternoon's bargaining with the rubber traders.

He alighted from his coach and progressed toward the
red brick building Mr. Quinton called home.

Victor Quinton's man servant smiled at Sebastian as
though he were glad to see him. He was. Stanley had
been with the Quinton family for many years, a family
retainer, and Stanley knew how bored Mr. Quinton had
become with the retired life. Not enough of the old gentleman's friends came to call, and Sebastian had always
been one of Mr. Quinton's favorites.

"Mr. Quinton has a caller at the moment, Mr. Rivera, but I am certain their meeting will end shortly.
Might you follow me into the drawing room and partake
of a glass of Mr. Quinton's brandy?"

"Yes, Stanley. I'd like that. A caller did you say?
Anyone I know?"

"I don't know, sir. I've not seen the lady before, although Mr. Quinton was beside himself when I announced her."

Resisting the impulse to impose on Stanley's friendship and cajole him into revealing the name of the caller,
Sebastian accepted the snifter of brandy and sat back to
light a cheroot.

Several moments later the door to the drawing room
swung open and Mr. Quinton in the company of Marilyn Bannon entered.

Sebastian's face turned dark and Marilyn's expression
mirrored it.

"Sebastian. How nice to see you! When did you get into
Manaus?" asked Mr. Quinton.

Sebastian answered his friend, his eyes on Marilyn.

"Ahem," sputtered Mr. Quinton. "Miss Bannon, may
I present Sebastian Rivera."

"Mr. Rivera and I have already met, thank you, Mr.

Quinton. How are you, Mr. Rivera?" she inquired in a flat voice.

"Well, Miss Bannon, and yourself?"

"Well."

A long silence followed, much to Mr. Quinton's bewilderment. One would have thought these two handsome people would find much to talk about.

"Mr. Quinton, thank you so much for seeing me today. You'll be hearing from me, I assure you," Marilyn said softly.

From where Sebastian stood, it seemed her golden-flecked eyes held a message for Mr. Quinton.

After Marilyn left, Victor Quinton joined Sebastian in a snifter of brandy. "I didn't know you knew Miss Bannon, Victor. You certainly are an old rake. I should have guessed you would know every lovely young lady that arrives in Manaus."

Victor Quinton's eyes grew serious as he measured Sebastian. "I'd like you to watch over her for me, Sebastian."

Sebastian almost choked on a swallow of brandy. "You can't be serious, Victor! Watch over her! Damned if I will!"

Shocked by this sudden outburst, Victor Quinton could only stare at Sebastian, mouth agape. "But surely you can do this for an old friend," he pleaded. "Certainly you are not one to refrain from the company of a beautiful woman?"

"I have been in Miss Bannon's company, Victor, and I have found her to be a lovely lady, although a devious one."

Sebastian went on to explain to Mr. Quinton the way he had met Marilyn. His lip curled in distaste as he described how he had felt himself deceived that Marilyn was a guest of Mrs. Quince. "I tell you, Victor, had I known she was traveling to the 'Tree' I would have cut a path a mile wide to stay away from her. And now I am given to understand she is part-owner in that den of unpardonable injustice to humanity."

"Sebastian, think of it. The girl has only been here a

matter of weeks. Surely you cannot blame her for the injustice that has run rampant on the 'Tree' all these
years. Consider it, please. That girl is within a hair's
breath of trouble. Judgment tells me she'll be in need of
a friend. And these sources that informed you that Miss
Bannon is part-owner in the 'Tree', have they also informed you that already the girl is trying the will of the
Baron in order that four children be permitted to return
to their parents? And have they told you of her disheart-
enment at the lot of the slaves on the 'Tree' and of her
guilt because of the fact that her life has been one of
ease and luxury at their expense?" Seeing Sebastian's
look of shame, Mr. Quinton softened his tone. "I knew
her father, Sebastian. Richard Bannon was a man to
your liking. He would never have allowed the deplorable
conditions on the 'Tree' if he had known of them. Take
pity on her, Sebastian, and me. Please watch over her."

"I'm afriad the damage is done, Victor. Miss Bannon
would no more encourage my friendship than she would
that of a snake in the grass."

"Perhaps," Mr. Quinton said, a knowing gleam in his
eye. "Nevertheless, you could be very unobtrusive,
couldn't you?"

Sebastian smiled and heaved a sigh. "I suppose I
could."

Marilyn leaned her head against the back of the seat
and rubbed a hand over her weary brow. So much, and
yet nothing. Mr. Quinton had revealed very little to her
about the mysterious words in her father's ledger. "Now
is not the time," he had insisted. But she had extracted a
promise from him to tell her something soon. She
thought of his round, kind face narrowing into deep
lines of concern. Why must men feel they have to coddle
women? Why can't they be honest and frank? Still, Mr.
Quinton had been most helpful in explaining the finer
points of her title, whatever that was. Even Mr. Quinton
could not be sure where the line was drawn. Tired, beat-
en—and then to meet *Sebastian* there! A small groan

escaped her and she forced back the frustrated sobs that
rose in her throat. A commotion in the street caught her
attention. Several blacks were erecting a papier-mâché
tower which was painted in garish colors. Carnival was
two days away and no one in Manaus felt less like cele-
brating than Marilyn.

# 10

Marilyn sat before the mirror putting the finishing
touches to her toilet.

A heavy tap sounded at the door and Mrs. Quince
strode briskly into the room. "Marilyn! Aren't you
dressed yet? The DuQuesnes are expecting us in thirty
minutes. You'll have to hurry or we'll be unfashionably
late!"

"I'm not going! You can tell the DuQuesnes for me I
have a very fashionable headache, and I'm afraid I cannot join them for still another night of revelry." Marilyn's tone was hostile.

"Child! What are you saying?" Mrs. Quince
squawked. "You cannot disappoint the DuQuesnes; the
table seating will be uneven, and I'm afraid it would
take another whole carnival season for Mrs. DuQuesne
to recover."

Marilyn could not keep herself from laughing. It was
comforting to know that Mrs. Quince also was bored
and disgusted by the endless supper parties of the elite
of Manaus.

"Mrs. Quince, you alone make this trying social parade bearable for me. Just to know your feelings are
akin to mine is what spurs me on and keeps me from
running back screaming to the 'Tree.' "

"I know, dear. Suzanne hated it, too. But, nevertheless, it is what is expected of us, and so duty calls." She sighed.

"How can you stand all this folderol every carnival season? I tell you, Mrs. Quince, if I have to look at one more gilt-edged anything, I will reward myself with a case of the old-fashioned vapors. These people are disgusting! Wherever did they get the notion that a bottle of heavy scent is a substitute for a bath?" Marilyn picked up a cut-glass bottle of scent and threw it on the bed. "I have sworn to myself never to wear perfumes and oils again. And the jewelry," she shrieked. "The Queen's own jewels are weak and lusterless compared to the rings and fobs the men wear! Let alone the geegaws with which the women adorn themselves! It's so ostentatious. I tell you, Mrs. Quince, I find it disgusting and repulsive!"

"I know, dear, but try to understand. These people are wealthy beyond imagination. Rubber has made them so. They have no outlet for their monies and frustrations aside from their homes and their garb. Try to pity them a little. If they were in America or France, their native countries, they would have no need for this display of money. But here, in the wilds of Brazil, it seems to bring them a feeling of security."

"Homes! You call these decorated mausoleums homes? I would sooner live in a thatched hut than in one of these painted, pretentious galleries of bad taste and worse art. The ceilings in the drawing rooms would rival the Sistine chapel for color and subject matter. Last evening at the Beaumonts I found myself eating my way through an orgy of an overseasoned, overcooked, nauseating, seven-course meal, while waiting for Mrs. Griswald's bosom to totally reject the bodice of her gown and come to flounder in the tapioca puddings, and all this took place under the sweetly smiling gaze of the painted cherub perched precariously on a stone pedestal above her head. It's disgusting, I tell you! I have never seen such indecent dress!"

"It *is* the latest style from Paris," Mrs. Quince said

pitifully as she patted her own curveless chest. "Oh, to be so well endowed," she sighed remorsefully.

"Oh, Mrs. Quince, how you do carry on!" Marilyn laughed. She glanced into the mirror at her own demure neckline which was somehow more seductive than the blatant, revealing décolletage of the other women.

She looked regal with her golden curls piled above her smooth brow. Her skin shone with health; the golden eyes complemented the deep sapphire blue silk of her gown.

As she was about to clasp a necklace about her slim neck, she thought better of it and instead fastened a small topaz brooch to her bodice. Satisfied with her appearance, she slid her narrow feet into a pair of sapphire blue slippers.

"Let us go, Mrs. Quince. We must not be unfashionably late to the DuQuesnes."

Mrs. Quince wore her most victorious smile as she left the bedroom with Marilyn.

"Mrs. Quince, could you come in here and fasten these little hooks for me? I can't seem to reach them," Marilyn called.

"In a moment, dear. I'm just about ready myself," came the reply.

Marilyn sat before her mirror winding the gold ribbon through her intricately braided hair. She and Mrs. Quince had left the DuQuesne dinner, as had all the other guests, to come back to the Quince's townhouse to dress for the carnival ball. "I'll never understand," she muttered to herself, "why they begin a ball at the ungodly hour of ten-thirty." A deep sigh escaped her; she was not looking forward to the festivities. She knew Sebastian would be there. "It galls me the way every woman in town makes cow eyes at him. One would think him a god of sorts." It didn't behoove her to think that her anger stemmed from jealousy. "Mr. Rivera this, and Mr. Rivera that," she continued, her sensibilities outraged, "and he sitting there basking in their fawning attentions. Disgusting!"

She could see him on the evening before last at the Roswells' dinner party, paying compliments to the Roswell's pudgy, dull, giggling daughter, and Mrs. Roswell beaming a satisfied smile toward the disappointed mothers whose own daughters shot covetous looks at Nancy. And Sebastian, enjoying it! Loathsome man! As if he could be interested in a dullard like Nancy Roswell.

And then to leave the poor lovesick girl to move to another, and no doubt regale her with the same practiced compliments he had paid to Nancy! Several times Marilyn had seen Sebastian glancing her way, and once he deliberately moved over to a circle of girls with whom she was talking and asked Cynthia Taylor to dance, greeting all in the circle save her!

Mrs. Quince entered the dressing room just then, finding the girl grimacing at her reflection in the mirror.

"Marilyn, what's the matter, dear? Don't you feel well? I know the sauce on the duckling was rich, but I swear I didn't see you take more than a bite!" Then, aware of Marilyn's dress, "Ah, I can see Anna has outdone herself with her needle . . . you're lovely, child, simply lovely!"

Marilyn reddened at Mrs. Quince's praise of her costume. She turned to face her reflection and appraised herself with unbending scrutiny. The soft white gown was empire in its lines, such as was so popular during the reign of Napoleon's Josephine. Gold ribbon outlined the severe V of the neckline and crossed over her bosom to wrap around her midriff several times over. The stark white of the shimmering silk was offset by heavy gold bracelets worn on her upper arm and complemented the gold kid slippers on her slim feet. In her hand she would carry a miniature bow and arrow.

Mrs. Quince's eyes swept from the top of Marilyn's golden head to the kid slippers on her feet. "I'm sure when the ancients spoke of 'Diana the Huntress' they never could have imagined one to be so beautiful as yourself."

"Mrs. Quince, you must stop referring to me as beautiful! I appreciate your kindness, but I am sure you are much too extravagant in your priase."

"Nonsense, child, when one gets to be my age, one has the privilege of speaking one's mind and posh and tother with all the amenities. You'd better be careful this evening; you'll find yourself in the midst of lovesick young men and irate old mothers, not that it would be such a surprise to you. I've seen the effect you have on the young gentlemen here in Manaus, and I can assure you, you'll not be lacking for partners this night!"

Rosalie Quince fumbled with the tiny hooks at the back of Marilyn's costume, giving the girl ample time to study herself in the glass.

Mrs. Quince was truthful in her judgment. Marilyn knew she looked well in Anna's handiwork. The dress accentuated her tall slimness, and the severe neckline revealed a bosom more ample than her spare form should allow.

"Marilyn, we'll have to hurry. Mr. Quince is downstairs waiting for us now." From there on Marilyn only half-listened to the angular, gray-haired lady whom she had come to love.

"That man," Rosalie continued. "One would think he had a clock for a brain. You know how he hates to be kept waiting."

Marilyn faintly heard Mrs. Quince carry on in this way until they had reached the top of the main staircase. Mrs. Quince suddenly became still and stood there beaming down at her husband, Alenzo. He stood at the foot of the stairs and gazed upward at his wife. It was not the first time Marilyn had been a witness to the love these two shared for each other. Alenzo Quince was a tall, pink-cheeked man with silvery white hair. His watery, faded blue eyes held a tenderness for his wife that was still evident after so many years. He clearly adored her and the feeling was reciprocated by Mrs. Quince. As they came down the staircase he lavished compliments on Mrs. Quince's choice of dress, a pale blue satin, and only as an afterthought did he think to compliment Marilyn on her costume.

Marilyn did not take this as an affront to her appearance. Instead she felt lighthearted, as always, at the steady, deep love that was shared between the long-married Quinces.

As they neared the vicinity of the Parradays' home, where the ball was to be held this year, the traffic of carriages came to a standstill.

"Oh, dear," remarked Mrs. Quince in a troubled tone, "and I am supposed to be on the receiving line. As a judge, it is one of my duties."

Alenzo Quince glanced at his wife and smiled, and Marilyn felt the unspoken recriminations of Rosalie's habitual tardiness.

"This could take some time, my dear. Perhaps if you do not feel it too far to walk, we could alight here. It is but a very short way."

"Alenzo, once again I marvel at your astuteness. Of course, we'll walk!" Marilyn could see this was just what practical Mrs. Quince would have suggested herself, but she allowed her husband to claim the idea for his own. Mr. Quince alighted from the coach and proceeded to assist his wife and Marilyn. While he was giving orders to the coachman, Marilyn turned to see Mrs. Quince give her a decidedly conspiratorial wink. The three then linked arms and strolled the short way to the Parradays'.

Several yards away from the front entrance, Marilyn caught sight of a tall familiar figure speaking furtively to a dainty, dark-haired girl. So involved was he in this conversation that Carl did not even notice her. As they passed the couple, Marilyn heard Carl say in a pleading voice, "Please, darling, please try to understand. The Baron demands this of me and I must comply. I'll be with you as frequently as I can. Please, dear, for my sake?"

The girl brought her handkerchief to her face as though she were brushing away a tear. Embarrassed, Marilyn wondered what Carl could have said that would make the girl cry. Then she found she was startled at the familiar terms he used, "darling" and "dear." Though she was shocked that Carl was apparently so involved with another girl when he had been paying obvious court to her, after a moment she found herself relieved that his heart would not break if the time ever came to tell him that she could never consider marriage to him. Still, there came again that slightly off-center feeling she had so often experienced at the 'Tree.'

She had no more time to think on it, as they were now approaching the bright lanterns that lit the entrance to the Parradays' palatial home.

Her eyes flicked over the crowd, and she noticed the Baron peering off into the distance searching the melee of carriages, no doubt searching for Mrs. Quince's party. As they came nearer he turned suddenly and saw her. He pushed his way through the throng and came over to her.

"Marilyn, how lovely you look!" He nodded his greetings to the Quinces, remarking on Mrs. Quince's choice of gown, and said, "I am sure you have duties to perform, Mrs. Quince. I shall see to Marilyn."

Mrs. Quince sniffed her acquiescence and went up the marble steps to the ball.

"Let us wait here a moment for the crowd to thin, Marilyn. I wouldn't want you to be trampled."

As he spoke in that smooth voice he took her arm, placing his hand not on her elbow, but slightly higher. Puzzled by this intimacy, Marilyn looked up at his handsome face questioningly. But the Baron acted as though there were nothing amiss and gazed down at her smiling. "You're beautiful. How fitting that you come as Diana. I have often equated your beauty with that of the goddess."

The people milled toward them in that instant, and Marilyn could feel the back of his hand pressing into the softness at the side of her breast. Alarmed, she glanced upward again, but the Baron had seemed to take no note of it—or had he? Little chills ran up Marilyn's spine, and she watched for the first opening in the crowd so that she could be free of the hot hand pressing against her so intimately.

The chance came and the Baron followed her up the steps, releasing her arm, much to her relief.

Inside, the ballroom was ablaze with gas lights. The great crystal chandelier suffused its light into shimmering beams on the ladies and gentlemen dressed in jewel-like colors. Off to the side of the ballroom, there were rows of chairs upholstered in crimson brocade, where the ladies could sit and watch the dancing. Opposite, there were two thronelike chairs ensconced with tropical flowers of all descriptions.

Within minutes her dance card was full, with the Baron claiming the first dance. Secretly she held one waltz aside, not daring to admit even to herself that Sebastian might claim it.

Carl approached her and was effusive in his compliments. There was nothing in his manner to betray the pleading attitude she had witnessed outside, in the shadows.

"I hope you have saved a waltz for me, Marilyn."

"Yes, Carl. I took the liberty to give you the third dance. If it's not convenient, I could change it."

"Quite convenient. Although I wish I could claim them all." Marilyn wondered if she could have been mistaken. Could it have been someone who looked like Carl outside the Parradays' not minutes before, someone else who had called the girl "darling?" No, she knew she had been correct; what she didn't know was the reason for his false attention. Why did he pretend to care for her? Just then, the Baron interupted her thoughts. "Every eye in the ballroom is upon you, Marilyn." Then, eyeing Carl disdainfully, "You are most fortunate, Carl, to have the loveliest lady as your partner this evening. I trust you can give her your full attention; you have settled that little problem, haven't you?" His tone was commanding and derisive. As if to temper his tone he bestowed a gleaming smile on his son. "But I believe, Marilyn, the first dance is mine, and as they are beginning . . . you will excuse us, Carl."

They stepped out onto the dance floor and took up their positions. The Baron held her around the waist and smiled down at her. The music began and she found herself whirling with the music across the floor. The Baron was a well-practiced dancer and she fell gracefully into the rhythm of the waltz. "Where is Jamie? I've not seen him this evening."

"He is here. We came together. Look, there he is, looking for you no doubt, to add his name to your dance card."

Marilyn followed the Baron's gaze and spied Jamie standing on the perimeter of the ballroom. He was garbed in a bright-red soldier's uniform, brass buttons and insignia gleaming in the light.

"I might have known he would dress as a solidier." Marilyn laughed up at the Baron, feeling much more at ease with him now that he had loosened his arm around her waist.

"Yes," the Baron smiled back. "As you can see, I don't care for the costumes; that is why I am wearing my dinner jacket. But Jamie wouldn't miss an opportunity to dress in costume. Ah, but such are the ways of the young."

Marilyn felt the Baron was leading her on and she rose to the bait. "But surely you don't consider yourself 'old?' I most certainly do not!"

Immediately he tightened his hold of her; he smiled down at her. "I'm glad you don't think so, Marilyn—so glad," he whispered meaningfully.

At once she became uncomfortable, remembering his intimacy with her just a few moments earlier. Disgust washed over her and she concentrated on the dance.

Carlyle Newsome led Marilyn across the floor, feeling her lithe form in his arms and reveling in the sensation. She was undoubtedly the most stunning creature he had seen in years. He had always like his women tall and Marilyn's stature was well above average. She made all the other women appear dowdy and frumpish if compared to her natural grace. He had watched her, studied her, compared her through the midst of the countless parties they had attended severally since carnival began. And always she carried herself with an ethereal poise and an air of sublimity. Damn fool, that Carl! Here he was, with the most beautiful girl in Brazil his for the asking, and he would prefer that mouse, Alicia!

As the Baron held Marilyn he felt a stirring within him, a familiar cord being struck. He wondered why it had never occurred to him to have Marilyn for his own. He was only slightly past fifty, not too old for someone as mature as Marilyn. Had she not said herself that she never considered him old?

Daringly, he held her close to him, and maneuvered her into the reverse position. As he dipped her backward, he could feel the soft protuberance of her breasts, feel her slim torso bend beneath him. He heard the sharp intake of her breath and misunderstood it for excitement.

When they had straightened he laughed softly at her and was startled to see her annoyance flush on her face. "Sir," she said sharply, "I do not reverse! It is unbefitting a lady!" Her golden-flecked eyes glittered angrily at him and he felt his ego deflate. There was no mistaking the dislike for him in her voice or the trace of disgust in her look.

Had they been anywhere but here he would have struck out at that disgust and changed her superior attitude to one of remorse and humility. She would be no longer smug with him when he had slapped her dignity from her and left her cringing at the mere sound of his voice. In that moment Carlyle Newsome hated Marilyn, his hate tinged with fear. She had caught him unawares and rendered a forceful blow to his image of himself as a man.

Suddenly, he threw his head back and laughed, drawing attention to himself from the other dancers. Let Carl have her; she deserves him, the thin-blooded New England miss that dared to demand an accounting of her inheritance. They deserve each other! The thought brought on a new burst of laughter from deep in the Baron's throat.

*He's mad!* Marilyn thought. *Hopelessly mad!* She had seen the cruel glittering in his gray eyes and it had frightened her. Before she could give it more thought, the music had stopped and she was being led by the Baron to Mrs. Quince.

Later in the evening Jamie approached her to claim his dance. He was resplendent in his costume and his courtly manner was impressive. Still, Marilyn could not help but remember the conversation she had overheard between Jamie and Elena, and Marilyn felt a certain qualm about dancing with him. She decided she was being silly and allowed Jamie to lead her out onto the dance floor.

Jamie danced surprisingly well and soon Marilyn was lost in the music. "When will you be coming home to the 'Tree,' Marilyn? I so miss your playing the piano." Marilyn was moved by Jamie's thinking of the 'Tree' as her home.

"I'll be home in a day or two, Jamie, as soon as Mrs. Quince has rested from her rigorous duties as judge. Mr. Quince does not want her to overexert herself. But it will be soon." She smiled up at him. Once again Marilyn was struck by Jamie's good looks. Sandy-colored hair, thick and glossy; strong, firm jaw. Whereas Carl was handsome, he was more the dandy, but Jamie had a rugged handsomeness, like Sebastian. She furtively glanced at Jamie again; yes, she thought she might have been mistaken, but no, there it was—a marked resemblance to Sebastian. Marilyn looked away quickly; she didn't want Jamie to see her looking at him in that puzzled way. Marilyn suddenly became angry, angry with Sebastian for his foolish attitude about his parentage, angry with Carl for his devious methods in courting her, angry with the Baron for his lewdness. She could well imagine how he had used Sebastian's mother and then tossed her aside. It had become as apparent to Marilyn as it had to other people that there was a very good chance that the Baron was Sebastian's father. Suddenly it dawned on her; could this be the reason the old Baron had disinherited Carlyle Newsome? It would appear the dates would coincide. From what she knew of her father's old friend, he would demand that Carlyle do his duty by the girl and, perhaps, because he had refused to do that duty, the old Baron had disclaimed him as his son. She meant to find out more about this mystery. "Tell me, Jamie, did you ever know your grandfather?"

"Oh, no. He died before I was born. It was just after father came back from England; that was where he met and married my mother, you know."

"I heard rumors, Jamie—" here she tread carefully— "that your grandfather had disinherited your father. How is it then that he came back into your grandfather's good graces?"

"Oh, I don't think he ever did gain the old man's good graces. Once Carl told me that father owns the 'Tree' because no other will could be found, and therefore all properties reverted back to the natural son." To Marilyn's knowing ears it sounded like another of Jamie's well-learned school lessons.

"But surely if your grandfather truly disinherited your father, the properties would not have reverted back to him?" Marilyn was testing his knowledge.

"Oh, I don't know, Marilyn. That kind of thing doesn't interest me. It doesn't seem real, somehow. But take my toy soldiers, they're real. I had this costume copied after one of my favorites. It's the kind the British officers wore during the Crimean War—" Noting Marilyn's preoccupation with his grandfather, Jamie offered, "I could take you for a ride over to see the old plantation if you like. It's not far from the new one. As a matter of fact, father copied it line for line, room for room. I think I told you this once before, didn't I?"

"Yes. But I would very much like to see the old ruins. There was a fire, I think you mentioned."

"Yes. It makes me sad to think of it. Grandfather died in the fire you know."

Marilyn's eyebrows shot upward, "No. I didn't. I just assumed he died from old age."

"Oh, no," Jamie's face turned a mite pale. "We Newsomes always die a violent death."

"Jamie! Who told you that?"

"No one. But I like to think it's true; then I could show everyone how brave I really am."

"Don't talk foolishness, Jamie."

"Well, it's true, Marilyn. Those little girls who wait on you think me a sissy, but I'll show them."

At the mention of the little girls, Marilyn's blood ran cold. The feel of Jamie's fingers on her back chilled her, and she was fearful of the determination in his voice.

Marilyn was very happy the music had come to an end. She was glad to be with Mrs. Quince, who could always be relied on to say what she meant. There were never any veiled meanings from that candid lady.

As Marilyn was escorted back to Mrs. Quince, she was pleasantly surprised to find the grand lady in conversation with Mr. Quinton, the attorney. At seeing her approach, Mr. Quinton stood and received her warmly.

"I don't want to interrupt, Mrs. Quince. You and Mr. Quinton seemed very deep in conversation. If it is something you wish to discuss privately, I'll excuse myself."

"Quite the contrary, dear," broke in Mr. Quinton. "Mrs. Quince and I were discussing you, as a matter of fact."

"Well, if that is the case, Mr. Quinton," demurred Marilyn, "I am sorry to be the cause of disagreement between you," she said as she glanced from one face to the other.

"Nonsense, child. It was merely that we don't agree on the time and place to tell you something that we both feel you have a right to know." The look on Mrs. Quince's face caused Marilyn some alarm.

"Whatever it is, I can see you consider it serious." Slowly she lifted her eyes to Mr. Quinton. "Is it what we discussed at your home earlier this week?"

"It is," came the brief reply.

"Well, as it happens, I was just discussing it with Jamie. I, too, think it abhorrent that the Baron has never claimed Mr. Rivera for his son; but since he has not, and Sebastian has inherited Farleigh Mallard's properties these many years now, I feel it a matter of beating a dead horse."

Abruptly, she turned on her heel to search for her next dance partner, leaving Mrs. Quince and Mr. Quinton with astonished expressions. As Marilyn searched the dance floor she could feel the heat burning her face. "I must look a sight," she thought. Well, she tried to excuse herself, it *is* like beating a dead horse. Why can't they just let it rest? All these reminders about his heritage cannot be comforting to Sebastian. Perhaps if they had been allowed to die years ago he wouldn't feel this rage toward the "Tree" and everyone on it. Including me, she thought sorrowfully. Another glance at the dance card told her that this was the waltz she had saved for Sebastian; but he had not sought her out to ask her to dance. Fresh anger boiled up within her, and she fled to the nearest balcony to escape the din of people around her.

On the balcony, overlooking the Parradays' extensive rose garden, Marilyn breathed deeply. The night air was exhilarating, so cool compared to the heat of the day. Almost at once she could feel herself relax, feel the strain of the past few days seep from her body. She leaned over the marble railing to reach out for a rose that had climbed up to the balustrade.

"Careful, better let me get that for you."

Marilyn spun around, almost losing her footing, to look into the dark eyes of Sebastian Rivera.

He casually reached out a long arm and captured the rose, plucked it, and proceeded to break the thorns from the stem. This gave her a chance to survey his costume. He was dressed in a black suit with a short snug-fitting jacket over a snowy white cambric shirt. A bright red satin band encircled his slim waist and topped off slim trousers. He wore a black sombrero at a rakish angle on his head, giving his square jaw emphasis.

"Here, I give you beauty without the barb."

"Is that supposed to mean something, Mr. Rivera?"

"Nothing personal, I assure you." His tone was condescending and she did not like it.

"Are you prepared for the evening before us, Miss Bannon?"

"Us, Mr. Rivera?"

"Yes. I understand you have been judged the most fair and therefore the queen of this ball."

Marilyn gasped. "How can that be? How do you know?"

"One has a way of finding out these things. Especially since Mrs. Quince warned me and gave me directives on how I was not to embarrass you with my surliness. I am to be a gracious partner and put aside all feelings, save those that are complimentary."

"You, why you?" Marilyn could not believe that Mrs. Quince had told Sebastian that she, Marilyn, was voted to be queen of the ball. On second thought she could if Sebastian was voted king. Lord a mercy! She hoped not. She could not endure his sarcasm for the rest of the evening. "Are you the king?"

"That is correct, Miss Bannon. I am to be your king. Pray remember to act surprised when it is announced. I know I can rely on your abilities as an actress."

"How dare you!"

"Oh yes, before I forget, do steer clear of Mrs. Roswell. It seems as though the dear lady exerted her pressure to have me be named king. Dear soul felt assured that her daughter, Nancy, would be named queen. A bit of matchmaking has been going on in the Roswell household, it seems. Anyway, when she hears you have been named queen, I am sure the fur will fly, as they say. And never fear, Miss Bannon. I assure you, you will find me the most attentive of kings."

"Oh you . . . you . . ."

"What? What am I, Miss Bannon?" He grabbed hold of her arm as it rose to strike him in the face. Marilyn was aghast that she could be capable of such an unfeminine action.

"Answer me, Miss Bannon, what am I? Am I a person to live off the misery of another human being? Am I? A little sarcasm would not be alien to you, I am sure. And as to being an actress—aren't you one, and a good one? Who would have supposed the day you went riding with me on my plantation that it was to distract me from the sabotage taking place elsewhere?" He held her arm in a fierce grip, squeezing till she cried out in pain. Immediately he seemed contrite and released her. She stood there, looking at him in disbelief, puzzled over his statement. Actress or no, he felt desire for her well up within him. Before either of them was aware, he had pulled her to him, crushing her lips beneath his in a tempestuous, burning kiss.

She fought him, pushing him away from her, feeling his burning lips above hers, lingering. She felt the brutality ebbing and something else taking its place, something demanding, sweet, yearning. With a will of its own, her body clung to his, her lips answering his demand. Without removing his mouth from hers, he sighed deeply; she could taste the wine punch he had been drinking, heady, tangy. She felt herself spinning as though in a whirlpool and Sebastian was her lifeline.

Roughly, he pushed her away from himself, his jet eyes peering deeply into hers. In a half audible groan she heard him murmur, "She-devil," and he pulled her to him for another kiss, this time more searching. When she felt herself stir in his arms he put her away from him, almost knocking her off her feet. She saw on his face a white, tight-lipped anger. Then he turned and left her alone on the balcony; the only sign that he had been there was the rose, crushed by his foot on the brick of the balcony as he made his hasty retreat.

Marilyn didn't know how long she stood there on the lonely balcony overlooking the rose garden. She was faintly aware that another dance was beginning and somewhere a young man would be searching for her to dance with him. She couldn't go in there, not the way she was feeling. At a sound behind her she turned to see Mr. Quinton.

"Here you are, my dear. I've been looking for you. This may be the last chance we have to talk before you go back to the plantation. There's something I must tell you."

Marilyn brought herself to her senses and could see that Mr. Quinton was struggling with indecision.

"Tell me, Mr. Quinton."

"It is most unpleasant, but Mrs. Quince assures me you have the mettle to take it."

"I think I do, Mr. Quinton."

"I am sure of it, Marilyn." He seemed to stiffen; he came closer to her and put a hand on her arm. "Your father was a friend, both of mine and the old Baron Newsome. Old Farleigh Mallard knew him also, and always had the kindest of words to say about him. I think a daughter of Richard Bannon's can listen to the truth and bear it."

He gazed at her with a stern expression on his face. Whatever the subject was he had to discuss with her, Marilyn knew it was most serious.

"Tell me, Mr. Quinton. I'm ready."

"Ahem. Yes. Remember you came to me and asked that I help you discover your rights as to the 'Tree of Life?' Yes, of course, forgive an old man. However, you also asked me about some cryptic phrases your father wrote in his journal concerning correspondence I had with him before his death. Now mind you, child, I have no proof; however, I wrote to your father that I had reason to believe that Carlyle Newsome, Jr., murdered the old Baron in cold blood and destroyed his will."

A gasp from Marilyn and a look at the shock written on her face distressed Mr. Quinton.

"I said I have no proof. However, it is my belief that this is so. I only tell you this, Marilyn, because I fear that if Carlyle would kill his own father to gain the 'Tree,' what might he do to you if you started to assert your rights as to your inheritance? Think on it, child. It is a matter of record that the Baron has frequently outspent his credit. His plantation could never earn what he spends in a year's time. Yet somehow he always manages to pay off his debts. Never mind the technicalities; it's simply this: I have reason to believe that Carlyle has been using your share of the estate for personal debts for some years now. Your poor father was given to believe that his share of the money was being vested in the plantation. According to the figures to which I have access at the bank as a trustee, this is not so.

"Please, child, hold off demanding an accounting of your shares till you hear from me. The situation you could place yourself in would be most dangerous."

Marilyn was about to speak in answer to the startling revelation when there came a scream and the sounds of hysterical people from within the ballroom.

"My God, what could be happening? It sounds like a revolution!" Mr. Quinton exclaimed.

The balcony on which they were standing followed the walls of the house, leading out to the front entrance from where the loudest cries were coming. Marilyn and Mr. Quinton hurried along the narrow balcony and came to a stop at the point closest the avenue. Below them was a scenario of horror. A coachman was settling his horses and trying to make them move backward. Beneath the deadly hooves was the small, crumpled body of a young woman. Marilyn watched, hypnotized by the gore. She saw Carl make his way through the crowd and come to bend over the battered body. It was the girl Marilyn had seen him talking with before the ball. His face was a grim mask as he bent over her; tears were streaming down his face, concern radiated from his stooped shoulders. Tenderly he stroked the poor little head, wiping away the smudges of dirt from her face. Marilyn knew then that Carl loved this girl, loved her with all his being.

A tall man came and put his hand on Carl's shoulder, trying to draw him away. Marilyn recognized the Baron. Carl stood up facing his father, his face twisted in a hideous expression of hatred. "You did this!" he shouted at the Baron. "You did this!" Unbelieving, Marilyn watched Carl reach out to strike the Baron. A man ran up and held him back. She knew if the blow had ever been struck the Baron would have fallen to the ground in a heap. Carl continued to shout, "You did this, you—" And then his emotions took over; tears streamed down his face, his shoulders heaved from his sobbing. "You

did this, damn you—and God help me—I helped you
do it!"

The milling of the crowd obscured her view of the
Baron. Why did Carl blame the girl's accident on the
Baron? Why . . . unless of course . . . Suddenly, it all
seemed hideously obvious—Carl's attentiveness toward
Marilyn, when he so evidently loved another; the times
the Baron suggested Carl take Marilyn for a walk in the
garden, or go riding or such. Marilyn felt her stomach
turn; she felt as though she would retch. It was all so obvious. The Baron wanted Carl to marry her so that he
would have full control of the "Tree." He rode over
Carl's emotions with no more concern than he would
have had were he crushing an insect.

Marilyn's heart cried out for Carl and she wished des-
perately she knew of some way to help him.

The crowd thinned and Marilyn watched the men
bring a door to carry the girl. Carl pushed aside all attempts by others to lift the poor broken body and he
tenderly lifted her onto the door himself. As he lifted
her, Marilyn saw a tiny movement in the girl's arm.
From where she stood it appeared the girl was reaching
out for Carl. She prayed the girl would live; she prayed
for Carl, but somehow she couldn't pray for the forgiveness of the Baron.


# 11


No sooner had the loud buzzing in the ballroom settled to a dull murmur when there were shrieks coming
from the open doorway. Marilyn turned to look at the
commotion and heard the word "Yellow Jack." Instantly, a man she did not recognize was surrounded by every

man at the ball. "It's on the 'Tree,' I tell you. I saw it
with my own eyes! They are lying on the ground and
dying."

"When did you see this?" asked a cold voice. It belonged to Sebastian Rivera.

"Two days ago. By now the situation is much worse."

Marilyn suddenly found herself standing next to Rosalie Quince. "We'd best start at once for the plantation,"
she called to her husband, Alenzo. He nodded and
strode from the room. The other men followed suit. Not
so Sebastian Rivera and the Baron.

"It is ridiculous," the Baron shouted, his face mixed
shades of crimson. "Who is this ridiculous person that
he can come in here to the biggest ball of the carnival
and start such a malicious rumor? I demand an explana-
tion," he said, grasping the man by the open collar of his
shirt.

"This is my foreman," Sebastian said coldly. "If he
says there is Yellow Jack on the 'Tree,' then it is true.
He knows what the fever is. He lost a mother, father,
and two children, not to mention a wife," Sebastian said,
his face a mask of fury.

Sebastian looked to the foreman. "And ours? What of
ours?"

"So far there is nothing. But one child is poorly. I do
not know at this time if it is going to be the fever or
not."

"Has the child been isolated from the others?"

"I saw to it, sir. It was the first thing I did," the man
answered.

"Good. Come, Jesus, we must leave at once. I don't
want to have to go through this again. Too well I remember the last time the fever struck. And you, sir," Sebastian said menacingly to the Baron. "Do you not plan
to return to the plantation? I think it would be best if
you did before the other plantation owners take matters
into their own hands. As you well know, we could be
wiped out in a matter of a few weeks. I warned you
many times, Carlyle, and you paid me no heed. This is

the result," he said ominously as he strode from the room.

Marilyn looked at the Baron; his face wore a mask of rage.

"How dare that bastard speak to me in such a tone."

Marilyn looked at the Baron in shock. How could he worry about so trivial a thing as the tone or the words another man uttered at a time like this?

"I will return to help," she said quietly.

"There is no need, my dear. I am sure all of this is nothing more than a start of some small uprising. And if there is some mild form of illness, then I am sure my own foreman and Elena can handle it."

"If that is so, sir, why then are all the others leaving? Evidently they are taking the whole matter quite seriously. And I, as half-owner of the 'Tree', also take it seriously. I will return immediately. You may do as you please, Baron."

Quickly Marilyn swept from the room and went in search of someone to drive the carriage to the plantation. There was, she felt, no time to be wasted in going back to Mrs. Quince's townhouse to change her gown. She would wear what she had on. She felt that time was more important. She had to leave, no matter what it cost her. Jamie joined her in the circular driveway.

"Do you think, Jamie, that with the both of us we could get back to the plantation? You are big and strong. Could you drive the carriage?" Jamie nodded dumbly. Quickly Marilyn rejected her own proposal and turned to see the Baron command the man standing by the carriage to get it in motion. "Leave for the plantation immediately." Wearily Marilyn climbed aboard and Jamie followed suit. The Baron settled himself comfortably and lit a cigar.

The journey was the next thing to unbearable. Marilyn was jostled and bounced from one corner of the carriage to the other. She was cold and hungry. She thought the journey would never end. Hours passed. All the while the Baron chatted with Jamie about matters of no importance. Marilyn gritted her teeth and thought venomously that if they mentioned toy soldiers one more time she would scream. Eventually the trip ended and she climbed wearily from the carriage and went in search of Elena. She was nowhere to be found. The beautiful house looked as though no one lived in it; there was a film of dampness and mildew over everything. In the large kitchens that were Elena's domain there was again no sign of life. A bowl of rotting fruit covered by flies rested on the stout wooden table. Marilyn suppressed a shudder. A loaf of bread with a huge knife buried in the middle of it lay next to the rotting fruit. It, too, was covered with a blue-yellow mold. Marilyn looked up to find the cold, penetrating eyes of the Baron eyeing the table.

For the first time he realized that the matter was indeed serious. Elena should have been here, and never in all the years that she had been the housekeeper had he ever seen rotting fruit in his house.

The Baron literally raced from the room and headed for the stables. Marilyn followed closely behind him. Jamie remained inside, the matter not concerning him. Quickly the Baron mounted and Marilyn did the same. She had never ridden without a saddle, but there was no one in the stable to help saddle the horse and she did not wish to waste any time.

As the heat beat down on her, Marilyn began to feel the strain of riding the large gray. Perspiration ran down her body and exertion caused her to gasp for breath. She had a difficult time remaining seated on the slippery back of the gray and held on for dear life. The Baron rode effortlessly. Soon they reined in the horses and Marilyn quickly slid to the ground. She looked around the clearing that housed the Indians and the blacks. Everywhere she looked there were pallets on the ground, and men, and women, and children moaned in agony. To the left, her eyes sought for and found the small burial ground she had noticed on her last visit. There were many more fresh mounds of earth now. She shaded her eyes from the hot sun and tried to count. There appeared to be twenty-seven. She blinked in disbelief. To the right of the burial grounds there looked to be a mound of something with a piece of canvas over it. She looked at Elena who had walked over to join the Baron. Noticing the look on Marilyn's face, she nodded. "There is no one to bury them. There is no one to dig the graves. The last of the men fell sick three days ago. I cannot do it," she said wearily.

The Baron looked around distastefully. "Is this the best you could do?" he asked frigidly, his upper lip curling at the stench of rotting flesh.

"How many of them are left?" he asked calmly.

Elena shrugged. "We lost as many as fifty and those," she said, pointing a finger to the far corner of the clearing, "can never make it. They are in the last stages. There is nothing to be done for them except to give them a little water from time to time and a cool cloth on their heads. These," she said, pointing to several huts behind her, "are the ones that just came down with the fever a few days ago. I am doing the best I can, Baron, but I must have some help or all of them will die. Perhaps Carl—"

"Carl? My son?" the Baron shouted. "Do you think I want him to get this filthy disease? Carl is not to set foot in this clearing. Is that understood, Elena?"

She merely nodded wearily.

"I'll help you, Elena," Marilyn said quietly. "If you tell me what to do I will be glad to do my share."

Elena looked at the tall blonde girl with the quiet golden eyes, looked at the elaborately coiled blonde hair, the gleaming Grecian gown, the long slender hands with the slender fingers and the unblemished skin. Again she nodded wearily as she let her eyes fall to her own dirty tattered clothing and the red, dry, cracked skin of her own hands. "Come," she said to Marilyn, "you can help with the children. I think there is hope for some of them."

"Is it Bridget and Rosy?" Marilyn asked fearfully.

Elena nodded. "Rosy, I am sure, will get well. Bridget is holding her own at the moment." She led Marilyn into the stifling hut. She looked down in the dimness at the two small figures on the straw pallets. Their eyes were bright with fever and their cheeks flushed, their lips red and cracked. Marilyn gathered up the train of the Grecian gown and tucked it under the gold girdle and knelt beside the two little girls. Gently she touched their cheeks. Neither child responded.

"It is time to give them a little water and they should be wiped down. Can you do this?"

Marilyn nodded and bent to the task. Elena herself rose from her knees and looked with unseeing eyes as the Baron rode from the clearing. She did not know what she expected from the man. Somehow she had thought he would help. Her shoulders slumped and Marilyn, looking up from the children, spoke.

"He would be worth nothing, Elena. He wouldn't know the first thing to do for these people. And he would only be in the way. I will help you, and I feel sure that Mrs. Quince will arrive here in a few days to help us. That is, providing that there is no fever on her own plantation. I will do all I can, Elena. I'll not shirk my share."

Marilyn was as good as her word. For four days and four nights she worked side by side with Elena as they dug fresh graves and lowered the decaying flesh into its final resting place. Her hands were blistered and raw and bleeding. She had long since shed the satin dancing slippers she had worn. Now she walked barefoot. Her feet were cut and bleeding from the rocks and the sharp vines. Her golden hair was tied back from her face with a stout piece of cord. She resembled a bedraggled street urchin. Her eyes were huge dark circles in her white face.

On the morning of the fifth day she was standing by the open fire making a weak broth for the sick when Rosalie Quince rode into the clearing. "Lord a mercy!" came the raucous shout. "Is that you, child? Yes, I can see that it is." Quickly she dismounted and wrapped her arms around the weary Marilyn.

"It is a losing battle, Mrs. Quince," Marilyn said, waving her hand around the clearing.

"I am here to help," Mrs. Quince said briskly. "Remove the broth and come over here and tell me how the situation stands."

Marilyn obeyed and quickly explained. Mrs. Quince nodded mutely. "I stopped by the Casa Grande and the Baron was roaring drunk. I wouldn't hesitate to say that he has been in that condition for some days now. Jamie was stomping the floor in some kind of a temper tantrum. Do you have any strength left, child?"

Marilyn nodded. "I am strong as an ox, Mrs. Quince. I can do whatever is needed. Just tell me what I am to do."

"Now this is what we are to do. First, we must burn everything. We will set fire to the lowlands and the marshes. I've brought some brave men from my plantation. They'll set up smudge pots. They've brought their drums with them. It's the fetid air that causes the fever. It just lays there all about us, calm and still." Rosalie Quince's face froze into deep, hard lines. Her eyes took on a faraway look, and she seemed to be steeling herself to pit her strength against an ancient enemy—the Yellow Jack. There were graves here in the damp soil of Brazil which Rosalie had dug herself. There was a baby —dead of Yellow Jack—whose small bones had fed the stinking roots of some strange tree.

Rosalie Quince visibly shook herself and brought her thoughts back to the present.

"But first we must do something about separating the sick ones. How many of them are vomiting blood?"

Marilyn spoke quietly. "More than a dozen, Mrs. Quince. Inexperienced as I am, I have noticed that those who vomit blood are the ones that we cannot help."

Within a matter of hours they had the sick separated to Mrs. Quince's satisfaction. Everyone was moved well to the back of the clearing. Mrs. Quince, herself, was hacking at the stout vines and dragging them into the jungles. "We have to have enough room for them when we start the fires."

Marilyn settled the children and tried to spoon some of the broth into Bridget. It ran down her chin and

caused her to choke. Immediately she started to vomit.
Marilyn looked in horrified disbelief. "God in heaven.
No, not the child too. She is so small. There must be
something I can do."

Agonized, she called Mrs. Quince. The lady took in
the scene and shook her head. "I know, child; that is the
way it is."

"There must be something, Mrs. Quince. Something.
Anything, I will do anything," she pleaded tearfully. "I
cannot believe that God would allow this to happen to a
helpless child," she said bitterly. "Surely, Mrs. Quince,
in all of your years in the jungle, there must be something you know that could be of help."

"Child, if there was, do you not think that Elena
would know? Some of these are her people, you know."

Marilyn nodded, wiping her eyes.

"Come, child. We have work to do. We cannot help
little Bridget now and perhaps we can save some of the
others. I know that it is hard, but you will find that in
time you will be able to accept this."

Marilyn shouted vehemently, "Never!"

The two women worked side by side the remainder of
the day. The heat from the roaring fires exhausted Marilyn and caused her to stumble and fall time after time.
She was soot-blackened from head to toe. By nightfall
the huts and the clothing had burned to cinders. The
marshes were still smoldering. By the light of the fire in
the middle of the clearing, Marilyn and Mrs. Quince
brushed the cinders and the rubble into a pile at the far
end of the clearing.

Marilyn swayed on her feet.

"Come, child. We must have something to eat. We
have worked long and hard. Tomorrow is another hard
day of work."

"Why do none of the other plantation people come
and help, Mrs. Quince?" Marilyn asked.

"They, too, have their problems. The rubber shipment has to be gotten out. Have you forgotten? They
are not callous, child; they have their own sick to take
care of. I came here because of you, child. We have but

two cases on our own plantation and they are on the mend. Alenzo can see to them. The Baron has been warned time and again that the conditions under which these people are expected to live make of this place a breeding center for disease. The Indians themselves are a clean people, given a chance. But they work sixteen hours a day in the rubber groves. They came here to eat and sleep. The food is insufficient to keep a body going. There's no energy left in them to care about their surroundings. Come now, let us have some of that broth you made earlier in the day."

"First I have to see Bridget. I intend to eat later, Mrs. Quince." The good lady merely nodded and sat down by the fire. She knew that Marilyn had to see to the child. She watched the tattered, golden girl wash her face and hands and walk into the hut. Marilyn remained inside for quite some time. Mrs. Quince looked thoughtfully around the clearing at their hard day's work and knew that the next day the work would be even harder. She knew there would be many graves to be dug. She prayed for the strength to endure and also for the slim girl who would have to work at her side. Elena possibly could help, but someone had to stay with the sick and the children. No, she and the girl would have to do it alone. She contemplated the future of the "Tree" with a sour feeling. How it could survive after this holocaust was beyond her tired brain. Truly, she was getting old. Every bone in her aging body ached. She was so tired. She reached for her pallet and drew it closer to the fire. She thought to rest only a moment till Marilyn returned. She closed her eyes and knew no more till she awoke in the morning hearing soft sobs. She looked around the now stark clearing and saw Marilyn carrying the small child in her arms, the tears flowing down her cheeks.

"I did everything I could, Mrs. Quince. Truly I did."

She stopped to wrap heavy green leaves around her blistered hands. Dejection was replaced by white-hot anger as the small hole began to grow larger. The dirt flew from the shovel. Mrs. Quince, spurred by the anger of her young friend, shoveled just as hard. Soon, that task complete, they lowered the small, still form into the ground. The dirt was replaced. The soft "thunk" of the earth on the unmoving bundle melted the tears, frozen till now within her, causing them to bubble to the surface. Rosalie Quince felt fury stir her as it had her young friend. "There must be an answer," she pleaded, looking heavenward. "There has to be an answer."

"Mrs. Quince, who is to tell the child's parents? They are on Sebastian Rivera's plantation."

"I will do it, child. But not now. We cannot leave here, as you well know. There is not a plantation in all of Brazil that would make either of us welcome at this moment."

The grim task completed, both women walked slowly back to the clearing. "I long for a bath and clean clothes," Marilyn said softly.

"Have you no other clothes with you, child? Cannot Elena go to the casa and fetch you clean garments?"

"I thought of that, but the Baron will not allow either of us to go near the casa; and he himself will not venture out of the door even to leave us something at the edge of the lawns. I fear he thinks he will be contaminated."

"The man is contaminated by many things," Rosalie Quince snorted, "and alcohol is at the top of the list. How many times have I heard the other plantation owners ask him and plead with him to clean up this place, especially Sebastian. This is what it has come to. All this suffering and wastefulness. All these lives lost for the selfishness of one man. I do not know how Carl could have not spoken up and at least tried to do something." She sighed at the hopelessness of the situation.

"That dress you have on reminds me suspiciously of the elegant gown you wore to carnival. Is it?"

"I am afraid so, Mrs. Quince. Come, let us have some fruit and then we had best get on with our work. I looked in on Elena before, and she was asleep and I did not have the heart to wake her. She is just as tired as we are. I checked everyone in the early hours. I fear we will lose three more before the day is over. There are six on the mend and I do think Elena was right—Rosy looks like she may pull through this, too. There is one old man that is now up and around. He has been helping Elena in a small way. But he has little strength and must rest frequently or he may suffer a relapse."

Once again Marilyn checked her sick patients and joined Mrs. Quince for some fresh mangoes. She sucked the juice from the rich, tart fruit but in truth had not the energy to chew the meat. Neither did Mrs. Quince, it appeared.

The two women trudged wearily to the lowlands and immediately started their small fires. Marilyn watched as myriads of mosquitoes swirled in the air. As they slapped the voracious insects away, the smoke billowed and swirled and seemed to devour the thick swarms of pests.

"Come, child. The fire will not spread, and if it should, where would it go? Only into the jungle. Come now." Marilyn stumbled over a low-slung vine. Gasping for breath, she lay for a minute, stunned after her sudden fall. Mrs. Quince helped her back to the clearing, fetched a small stool for her, and helped her to rest for a moment. "Let me see your feet, child. God in heaven, what has happened?" She looked at the cuts and the welts, and the deep scabs that were cracked and oozing blood. "Wait here and do not move."

She was back in minutes with Elena. She pointed to Marilyn's feet and the housekeeper gently inspected one. Horror danced across her face. "Why did you not tell me of this?" she asked quietly.

"We had enough problems without my feet being added to the list." Marilyn smiled. "They do not hurt much now. I have been so busy I have not had time to think of the pain. Please don't worry, I beg of you. The others need help. I will be all right. How are the old lady and her daughter?"

"Both gone, this past hour."

Marilyn rose to her feet and grasped the handle of the shovel. "If you and Mrs. Quince can carry the bodies, I will do the digging. You know we cannot let the bodies stay in this abysmal heat."

Marilyn felt each shovelful of earth would be her last. But somehow, from somewhere, she garnered the strength. She kept thinking of all the goods that money from this plantation had bought her. At each new item on the list she got renewed strength. She would shovel till it killed her, and it probably would, she thought grimly. She would pay for it all. She did not stop to think, nor did she care, that the suffering was not her doing. She knew that she had to make up for the sins of Carlyle Newsome.

When the bodies had been lowered into the shallow grave Marilyn rested a moment before she tackled the mound of earth. She swayed and prayed for the strength to finish the task before her. As she looked at the mound of earth in front of her it took on gigantic proportions in her eyes. She must do something. She could not faint now. She grasped the handle in her bleeding hands and, muttering under her breath, she dug the shovel into the soft, rancid-smelling earth.

This is for the costly dancing lessons, and the filigree comb, and the yellow satin ballgown that I nagged father to buy me, and for the matched set of pearls—they alone would be good for many shovelfuls, she thought tartly, a pearl for a shovelful of earth. It seemed a fair settlement. How many pearls were there on the strand? For the life of her she could not remember. The strand was quite long—at least fifty. She would never wear those pearls again. Shovel, don't think, shovel, shovel, pearl, pearl, shovel, pearl. Lord, she thought, she must have shoveled fifty pearls by now. She wiped the perspiration from her face with a dirty, grimy arm, and streaks of blood from her torn and battered hands appeared on the creamy skin. She again looked at the mound of earth at her feet. It had diminished slightly. Mrs. Quince was now helping her and so was Elena. Just keep shoveling, remember the pearls. If you stop, you can never atone for the pearls. Just shovel.

When the last shovelful of earth was thrown, Marilyn tried to straighten her cramped and stooped back. She felt a million years old. She grasped the shovel in the crook of her arm and hobbled behind Elena and Mrs. Quince. Her numbed brain and eyes watched the angular form of Mrs. Quince falter and stagger. She could not have reached out to her if her life had depended on it.

Back at the clearing, Elena brought a bowl of broth to the two women and again went to her nursing. Marilyn tried to hold the bowl but could not get her hands to obey her commands. She peered at their raw flesh with interest and marveled at the fact that she experienced no pain from them. She grasped the bowl with her wrists, which was a feat in itself, and drank thirstily. The bowl slipped and she made no effort to retrieve it. She looked at her tattered, bedraggled gown that was nothing more than strips of rags. It was in strips up to her knees. She was so weary she could barely keep her eyes open. She wished that she could sink into merciful oblivion and suddenly wake to find this whole thing had been nothing more than a bad dream.

"I must do something about my hands, Mrs. Quince. What do you think?" she asked, rising from the small stool she had been resting on. The bright sun beat down on her head and she swayed, sickened by the heat. She turned at the sounds of approaching horses. She tried to shade her eyes from the sun but the effort was too great. She stood silently till the riders came into view. Mrs. Quince at her side was equally silent.

There was a hoarse shout and what seemed like a roar from a bull elephant. Marilyn had the impression of a dark form standing in front of her. She tried to raise her eyes but the strong sun beat down unmercifully.

"Sebastian! Is it you? What in the world are you doing here?" Mrs. Quince gasped.

"I saw the smoke from my plantation. I knew things must be bad over here if you had resorted to the fires. Tell me, what is there for me to do?"

"Nothing I am afraid, Sebastian. It is too late for anything to be done. Marilyn and Elena have done it all. I just arrived yesterday."

Why is she babbling like that? Marilyn wondered wearily. Why doesn't she just be quiet and let him see for himself?

Well, he had been right. Now all he had to do was say I told you so. She waited for the stinging words. Finally she raised her tired eyes and looked at the tall man before her. She wanted to tell him something. What was it? She couldn't think. Tired as she was, she was again struck by the handsomeness of the man. She made a vain effort to squelch the stirring of her pulses. Of all the times in the whole wide world to have him see her, he had to pick today. She looked again at his cold dark face. She thought she must be delirious at what she read in his face. She was overtired. He couldn't possibly love her, yet it was a loving look he bestowed on her. She heard the outrage he shouted to the still air.

"Oh, do be quiet, Mr. Rivera. Do you not know there are sick people here? If there is one thing we do not need it is noise," she said in a whisper. She swayed as she spoke. Suddenly she was enfolded in strong arms and held close to a warm, hard body. Never in her life had she felt so safe and secure. What a blessed moment; don't let it end, she thought. She opened her eyes and gazed into the jet-black pools of Sebastian Rivera's eyes. I love him, she thought. I love this man who is holding me in his arms. And he loves me. *Wishful thinking, Marilyn,* she thought to herself as she closed her eyes. No longer could she ward off the badly needed sleep and rest her body now demanded. What better place to succumb than in the arms of the man she loved?

She felt her body being lifted gently. Vaguely she heard muttered curses of outrage. Who was doing the cursing she did not know, nor did she care. "Let me sleep, let me alone," she whispered over and over. They paid her no heed, these nameless voices and hands that were ministering to her body. What had she been dreaming about? A love, that was it. A love that knew no bounds. "Yes, I love him, I love him," she whispered

to herself. I love the tall dark man who held me so safe
in his arms. There was something she had to tell someone; what was it? She couldn't remember and she
moaned at her inadequacy. "Rest now," she heard a
voice command her.

She tried to open her eyes to see who was speaking to
her. She succeeded in opening the golden eyes to mere
slits and saw Sebastian Rivera looking down at her. He
smiled such a gentle smile she was sure she must be
dreaming. It had been such a long time since she had
seen him smile. Not since the riverboat.

Prior to his thunderous ride into the 'Tree," Sebastian had paced on the tile floor of his casa. White-hot
anger gripped his chest as he watched the billowing
smoke rise above the "Tree." To think that one imbecile
could wreak such havoc and still expect the other plantation owners to say nothing made Sebastian angry beyond belief.

Sebastian looked across at the grim face of his foreman, Jesus, and again felt a pang of pity for the man.
He had lived through the fever and lost everything he
held dear. To ride into it on someone else's plantation
and see the death and the suffering must be causing him
untold sorrow. There was no excuse for it. Neglect and
filth were the cause of the situation.

So far they had been lucky. There were only a few
cases on the other plantations. The owners had followed
his advice and cleaned up the lowlands and the marshes.
They had also paid him heed when he explained about
the sanitary conditions. And today they were not sorry.
Many of the owners had thanked him in the past few
days—all, in fact, but Carlyle Newsome. A poor excuse
for a man if there ever was one. His son, Carl, could
have, and Sebastian believed, would have stood on his
own feet and become a man if the Baron had not pulled
the purse strings. Sebastian winced as he recalled the
day he had offered Carl a position on his plantation. As
he had read the joyous hope and the mixture of grati-
tude and friendliness, he also remembered the despair

that replaced it so quickly. Carl could not leave the "Tree," his roots, such as they were. Sebastian had understood and reminded Carl that should the day ever arrive when he felt the need to leave he would always find a welcome at his plantation.

The jungle was so silent Sebastian felt uneasy. Gone were the raucous cries of the birds. Not a leaf moved. It was ominous. Great black columns of smoke whirled upward. As they rode into the clearing, Sebastian took in the scene in one swift glance.

It couldn't be. That beautiful golden angel from New England was no more. In her place he saw a filthy, tattered, soot-blackened witch. Hair once golden was now dirty and gray and hung in limp, bedraggled strands; part of a dried vine hung over one bare, grimy shoulder. Rage boiled up in him once more as he watched the dirty creature raise a torn bloody hand to shade her eyes. A sound roared from him as he leaped from his mount to catch her as she swayed. He held her soft pliant form and felt a wave of pity engulf his body. The equally grimy Rosalie Quince took matters into her own efficient hands and immediately gave him a brief description of the past days and of the accomplishments of Marilyn and Elena.

Sebastian looked at the soft face of the girl he held in his arms. As he inspected her bleeding hands and cut, oozing feet with their open sores, Sebastian swore viciously. Quickly he issued a terse command to Jesus, and the man rode from the clearing as if the demons of hell were at his heels. Within an hour there appeared at the clearing his own housekeeper and several strong Indians. Sebastian, holding Marilyn in his arms, issued commands like the man of action he was. All listened quietly, then sped to obey him. Marilyn was lowered gently into a wagon, and Rosalie Quince and Elena wearily climbed in with the help of Jesus. Sebastian took the reins and started for his plantation. He would kill someone, he was sure of it. His mind and body held such an alien feeling he could not put a name on it. He remembered his mother telling him once that when one fell in love there was no other feeling in the world like it. Sebastian would have staked his life on the fact that he had experienced every emotion there was. If so, what was this crawling, creeping feeling that threatened to engulf him? He wanted to kill, to make love, to fill his belly, but he could do none of these things. All he could do was drive this blasted wagon and let his mind have its way. Helpless, that's what he was. Never in his life had he been rendered helpless. His agile mind flitted like a bird. He kept stealing glances behind him at the girl on the wagon floor. Again he thought of his mother and her wise sayings. He tried to force the thoughts from his mind. He did not want to think of love and its ties and bindings. He did not want to give his soul to anyone. He wanted to own himself. What was it his mother had said? To love is to consume the other, or words to that effect. He cursed under his breath and began to drive the wagon even harder over the rutted ground, but the moans from the golden girl as she rolled from side to side made him slow down.

As he reined in the horses, women came. Sebastian was pushed gently out of the way while the slim girl was carried inside and the doors were closed to him.

"Go, Sebastian. You will just be in the way," Rosalie Quince shrilled. "This is women's work. Go smoke a cheroot or something."

"A cheroot," Sebastian said stupidly.

"Good Lord, Sebastian. Must I tell you again or should I draw you a picture?" she shouted briskly. "If we should need you we will call you. You have my word."

Sebastian nodded meekly, as he obeyed the business-like Mrs. Quince. He felt like a small boy again at his mother's knee.

The endless days crawled by on tortoise legs and slowly became weeks as Marilyn lay in a fever, delirious. Sebastian felt both mentally and physically exhausted. He had walked innumerable miles, pacing the wide veranda. His throat felt white hot from the countless cheroots he had smoked during his frantic pacing. From time to time his eyes smarted; no doubt from the thick cigar smoke, he told himself.

He flung himself wearily onto one of the rattan chairs and absently stroked the silky ears of the dog that lay at his feet. His touch was gentle and soft. The animal whined in pleasure. Suddenly Sebastian's gentle caresses ceased as he looked up and saw the angular form of Rosalie Quince towering over him. In his haste to get to his feet his movements were clumsy and he stepped on the dog's paw, causing the beast to yelp in pain. Rosalie Quince found it hard not to smile at this awkwardness. She had never seen the debonair Sebastian anything but graceful and completely at ease.

"The child is out of the woods, Sebastian. The fever has finally broken. I tell you now that if she had contracted Yellow Jack she would no longer be with us. How she escaped it is beyond me. The poor thing was just worn out. She's on the mend, Sebastian, so you may go about the plantation business." Shrewdly she watched the tall, tired man fling the chewed-up cheroot over the railing.

"That is good news, Mrs. Quince." Jet-black eyes looked questioningly at the tall lady, but no words were spoken. Mrs. Quince also remained silent. Their eyes locked in a stare. Would he ask to see the girl, Mrs. Quince wondered.

Should I ask to see the girl, Sebastian wondered. No, she was out of danger, and too long he had been absent from his many duties on the plantation. Sensing Mrs. Quince's thoughts, he smiled crookedly and strode from the veranda. Tonight he would leave for town; he would return by mid-morning of the following day. One could not fool oneself for long. And if there was one thing he prided himself on it was not being a fool. He contemplated the tearful Aloni when he would tell her, as gently as possible, that their relationship must come to an end. He would soften the blow with a generous settlement. He wouldn't fool himself. Aloni, he knew, was more interested in the comforts he could afford her than she was in Sebastian.

Marilyn's recovery was rapid. Mrs. Quince spoon-fed her till she regained her strength. Within ten days she was up and about and feeling stronger by the day. She had not seen Sebastian once since the fever had broken. She did not ask for him at all. She accepted the hospitality he had extended and wished only to thank him. Something always prevented her from asking for him. Mrs. Quince herself was careful not to mention his name. Marilyn wondered why.

It was the eve of her departure for the "Tree." Sebastian's foreman was to drive her there in the wagon and then take Mrs. Quince to her own plantation.

Marilyn dressed carefully for dinner in the hopes that Sebastian would arrive. She took great pains with her toilet. She still looked pale, but she felt she would pass muster if one did not look too closely. Rosalie Quince watched her in amusement as she carefully patted her own wiry, springy curls.

As the dinner hour approached and there was no sign of Sebastian, Marilyn felt almost sick. Not to show up for dinner! He was making a witling of her. She watched from the corner of her eye as Mrs. Quince looked all around.

"It appears we dine alone this evening, Mrs. Quince." Marilyn smiled brightly. I will not show that I care, she thought grimly. These hot-blooded Brazilians were sadly lacking in good manners. She with her blue blood, as they claimed, had indeed been brought up with good manners. And she would use them. Hadn't her father once told her in her early childhood that when one is hurt by the cruel taunts of another child, smile brightly as if nothing happened? Always put your adversary at a distinct disadvantage; then he has nothing further to gain by taunting. Marilyn would apply this rule now.

"I am positively ravenous, Mrs. Quince," Marilyn bubbled. "I can hardly wait till morning to leave. I want nothing more than to be back at the 'Tree!' I have sorely missed Jamie and the plantation. I cannot wait to see the condition of things. Do you know something, Mrs. Quince? I think when I get back I will spend more time with Jamie. And the little girls, perhaps I can also help them with some of their letters and numbers. Yes, I would like that," she continued to babble. "Rosy is so quick and bright. I also think she has a flair for drawing. I once saw her draw a magnificent castle. When I asked her where she saw such a thing she said she had seen it in one of Jamie's old books. Don't you think that is wonderful, Mrs. Quince?" Not waiting for a reply she continued to ramble on and on.

The usually articulate Mrs. Quince found she could not add one word to the conversation. She merely nodded from time to time at the brightly chattering girl. She did not miss the fact that the "ravenous" Marilyn only pushed at the food on her plate. If she ate two bites she would have been surprised. The meal over, Marilyn suddenly felt deflated. She felt she could not utter one more word. God in heaven—how did Mrs. Quince talk so much? Maybe it's her long, skinny neck, Marilyn marveled. As she pushed back her chair she heard footsteps approach the dining room. A warm flush stole up her neck and covered her face. So! He arrives now! Well, let him arrive now, for I am leaving.

Marilyn looked up and felt her pulses begin to pound at the mere sight of the tall dark man in front of her.

She spoke first. "Good evening, Mr. Rivera. I am most happy to see you this evening. I did want to thank you personally for the hospitality you have shown me during my illness. I will not soon forget it," she said, her tone cool. She tilted her head in a brief nod and walked gracefully from the room.

Back in the small room that had been hers for the stay, she collapsed on the bed and let her tears flow freely. *You will not, Sebastian Rivera, make a fool of me. It shall be the other way around.* How dare he show up after dinner and act like she was some stranger that had just dropped in! It was a small wonder he did not offer me one of those odious cheroots he smokes. She had never been so insulted in her life.

And Mrs. Quince, silent for the second time in her life, had stood by silently, like a wart on a frog. Sudden-

ly Marilyn laughed at the sight. There was poor Mrs.
Quince with a large wart on the end of her nose, gracefully smoking one of the foul cheroots. And Sebastian,
what was he doing? Why he was just standing with his
mouth hanging open and looking like a horse's rear end.
Marilyn broke into fresh laughter, doubling over on the
bed.

As Mrs. Quince and Sebastian walked down the corridor, they heard the happy laughter and looked silently
at each other, busy with their own thoughts.

"Sebastian, I have only one thing to say to you and
that is that you are a fool," she said sourly.

Sebastian raised startled eyes and frowned at the
sharp words.

"Spare me from foolish men in love. You are all jack-
asses," the good lady all but snarled.

"Who's in love?" Sebastian almost stammered.

"Who? Who? You ask me who? Get on with you! If I
have to tell you that, then there is no hope for the likes
of you. Go! I do not want to see you again for many
weeks. I cannot abide a fool in either long or short
pants."

"What have short pants to do with it?" Sebastian
muttered.

"When you were a small boy in short pants, that was
time enough for acting the fool. Now that you wear long
pants you should have outgrown all of your foolish tend-
encies. Begone!" she shouted imperiously.

As Sebastian strode down the long corridor he looked
at his legs. He would have not been surprised to find his
legs naked. He did feel the fool. Angrily he headed for
the stables. Perhaps a ride in the night air would help
him to think clearly. His head felt like a beehive.

# 12

Time passed slowly for Marilyn once more on the "Tree." For some reason Jamie seemed to avoid her. Carl was not in evidence, and Elena had warned her not to mention his name to the Baron. As for the Baron, he was never at home. After the disease had broken and the alcohol had run dry he had left for his townhouse and not returned. The lessons she had anticipated helping the little girls with did not materialize. With the death of little Bridget, the children seemed to want to do nothing but sit and stare at each other. They did not play or laugh. Marilyn was quite at a loss as to what to do. She felt that in time they would regain their natural, happy attitudes. She fervently hoped so.

One day, weary of sitting on the veranda, Marilyn decided to stroll through the gardens. She watched the birds as they flew overhead and listened to their shrill cries. Something bright caught her eye as she rounded the drive. Could it be one of the children? What were they doing? They were supposed to be cleaning the bedrooms; she had heard Elena giving them their instructions. Possibly they were taking a few minutes off. Carefully, lest she make some sound, she crept up behind the tall bush that now shielded the bright color. She looked and blinked: Jamie was throwing a ball and Nessie was obediently catching it. Rosy stood quietly watching. Jamie was smiling and happy. Not so the two small girls. They almost looked afraid. Suddenly Jamie shouted and grabbed Nessie by the arm. "I thought you liked to play ball," he shouted as he released her arm. He was getting angry.

Suddenly she was afraid for the little girls. What was the matter with Jamie? She backed away from her hiding spot with trembling limbs and silence greeted her as she called out, "Nessie! Rosy!" Quickly she walked into the small clearing and her glance took in the three figures who were standing as if carved from marble. Quickly Marilyn started to babble. "There you are," she cried. "Elena has been calling for you, girls. Best run along before she gets angry." Marilyn smiled grimly and watched the small girls run as if on winged feet. She heaved a heavy sigh and looked at Jamie. He was rubbing his fingers nervously. Apprehensively Marilyn watched him as she started from the small clearing. Jamie followed her, suddenly his old self.

"You must be feeling much better, Marilyn," Jamie said, "for you to walk out in this midday heat."

"Oh, I do feel so much better. But in truth, Jamie, I find myself very bored. There must be something for me to do to occupy my time." Is this then to be my lot in life? she thought sourly. To sit on the veranda, sleep, eat, and wait each year for the carnival? She looked at Jamie irritably and said just as irritably, "I wish I were back in New England."

"Why?" Jamie asked bluntly.

"There is nothing for me here in the jungles. I have made no friends and I also fear I will never get used to this infernal heat. There also many things I do not understand about this plantation and the operation of the rubber market. I feel I should know, yet your father chooses to keep me in the dark on such matters."

"The running of the plantation means work, Marilyn. Do you agree?"

"Of course, I agree," she said practically. "You were not listening to me, Jamie. I said I wanted to know about the operation. I did not say I wanted to run it. I want your father to give me an accounting of my monies and for some strange reason he does not want to do this. Do you have any ideas as to why he avoids my questions and even my demands?"

Jamie shrugged his broad shoulders. "Do not ask me anything of my father. He does not take me into his confidence and he did not take Carl into his confidence either. Time," he said, "will be the answer to everything."

Marilyn shivered in the moist, clammy heat of the day. An ominous feeling came over her. If asked to explain it she would have been at a loss. She stole a quick look at Jamie. His natural good humor appeared to be restored. She shivered once more as he smiled at her.

Once again on the veranda, she picked up the now warm drink. She winced at the sour taste and decided to go into the kitchen to ask for a more cooling drink.

Elena looked up from the fruit dish she had been preparing. She smiled at Marilyn and offered her a slice of guava. Marilyn shook her head and asked for the drink.

"Elena, I wish to speak to you of something that has been bothering me." At the sudden veiling of the housekeeper's eyes Marilyn wondered how she could know what she was about to ask. Quickly, before her courage could desert her, Marilyn explained what had happened in the clearing. "I don't think it wise for the children to play with and amuse Jamie. Does he have nothing to do but play with the children?"

"You realize that our customs here in Brazil are quite different than those in New England."

"Customs do not enter into this, Elena. It is a question of safety for the girls. Jamie was not himself today. What if I were not there? He could have hurt Nessie. I trust, Elena, that you will speak to Jamie about this. I would not want anything to happen to the children."

Elena inclined her head to one side. "I will speak to Jamie, Miss Bannon. Here is the drink you requested. Send Jamie to me on your way out. I believe he is on the veranda."

Marilyn delivered the message from Elena and sat back on the rattan chair. She closed her eyes wearily and wished she had someone to talk to. Suddenly the sound of a door slamming caused her to sit erect. Jamie strode onto the veranda and stood with clenched fists. He was again agitated. Marilyn stirred nervously. Jamie strode to the far end of the veranda where he had his soldiers lined on the rail. He neither by glance nor word acknowledged Marilyn's presence.

Marilyn watched in silent horror as the muscular man slowly and methodically began to snap the heads from the brilliantly uniformed soldiers. As each small head rolled to the floor it made a soft plunking sound. Mesmerized Marilyn silently began to count the small heads that rolled to the floor. His motions up to this point had been slow and careful. She could sense rather than see the tautness of his muscles bulging beneath his light coat.

Suddenly fury seemed to take hold of him. More and more quickly he snapped the small heads.

Marilyn looked at the rail and counted seven. There were only seven soldiers left! Quickly their heads were also severed. God in heaven! Marilyn raced into the kitchen for Elena. Swiftly she told the housekeeper what had happened. The housekeeper's eyes widened in shock. She followed Marilyn to the veranda and saw the severed heads on the floor, but there was no sign of Jamie.

"Elena," Marilyn demanded. "Where are the children?"

Elena looked blank for a moment. "Moriah is upstairs, doing the bedrooms. But Rosy went to fetch water from the spring and Nessie is disposing of the trash. They left together." Both women looked at each other. No longer were they mistress and housekeeper but two women, both anxious and upset at these new developments. "Come, we must find them," Elena exclaimed worriedly. "Follow me, Miss Bannon."

They ran to the small spring and then to the trash pile. Neither child was to be found. They retraced their steps to the large kitchen. There was no pail of water. The bucket that held the trash was also conspicuously absent. Again both women's eyes met.

Jamie ran down the veranda steps and around the side of the house. He would ride the way his father did.

What did I do, he wondered, to receive the tongue-lashing Elena gave me? She had never spoken to Carl like that. Wait till she sees what I did to the soldiers, he thought angrily. Then she would even be more angry. He did not care. They were his soldiers and he could do whatever he pleased. He wondered which one of the little brats had spoken of the ball playing. What was wrong with playing ball? It was all Nessie's fault. When he got his hands on her again he would give her a good slap. He didn't like Elena to be angry with him. Suddenly he looked up and spied Nessie and Rosy heading for the spring. Here was his chance. He would give it to her for getting him in trouble with Elena. Mouthy little brats. As he started to follow the girls, his heavy footfalls alerted the girls. They stopped dead in their tracks and waited as he called to them. Jamie looked at their dark faces and, suddenly unsure that his earlier choice was correct, wondered which one had told on him.

"Who spoke to Elena?" he demanded, his voice shrill. Neither child answered him, their eyes wary. "If you do not tell me I will give you *both* a thrashing you won't soon forget." The children remained silent. Their very silence only added to Jamie's anger.

Suddenly furious, he reached out a long arm and grabbed Rosy to him. "I'll teach you to tattle on me, you little brat," he roared. With one hand he held the child firmly by the arm, and with his free arm he gave her a resounding slap on the face. The child started to cry and to try to get out of the viselike grip. The more she struggled the more incensed Jamie became. Her frantic movements were driving him crazy with a strange feeling. Blinded by his emotion, he held firm to the child, whose writhing now seemed almost sensuously rhythmic to Jamie.

Fire grew in his loins. He looked at the small tearstained face of the wriggling child and felt tears of his own spring to his eyes. What was happening to him? A small dark hand reached up to claw at his face. He cursed as he felt the flesh split across the cheekbone. The fire was now approaching an inferno. He threw the child on the ground and stood looking over her. The inferno threatened to engulf him. He had to release the flames that burned within him now. He lunged toward the terrified child, stumbled, and fell on top of her, moaning with ecstasy.

Somewhere, from the dark recesses of his mind, he recalled standing with his father beside the stable's studding corral. He could see himself, a thin young boy of twelve. He could hear the shrieks of the mare and the snorts of the stallion as the two beasts commenced the act of mating. He remembered his father's soft laugh as he remarked to one of the stable hands, "She screams like a woman, that filly. The stallion will soon teach her to act her age."

But the filly never stopped screaming. Jamie could hear her now—or was it Rosy?

It seemed hours later when he staggered to his knees. Jamie looked around the now silent clearing and suddenly remembered. He looked overhead, thinking he had slept. He straightened his clothing and headed for the stable. He knew full well that when he returned to the house Elena would have another tongue-lashing for him. Besides, what was there to do at the house? He had ruined his beloved toy soldiers. There was no reason to hurry home. He pulled at the horse, none too gently. Quickly he saddled the mare and mounted. Without a backward glance he rode from the stable and into the jungle. He did not feel like sticking to the trails today. He was old enough to go where he wanted to. He was no child. Had he not just committed the act of manhood? He giggled to himself as he thought of the child. He sobered instantly as he then thought of Elena. Petulantly he pulled on the reins as he felt the horse try to take its head. He spoke soothingly to the horse and tried to quiet him. Something was bothering the animal. "Oh, all right," Jamie sulked as he loosened the reins. The huge beast immediately bolted, throwing Jamie off-balance. He felt himself slip from the horse; but unable to free his left foot of its stirrup, in a very short time he was being dragged by the bolting animal. His hands flailed at the nearby branches of the lush jungle undergrowth. Too late he saw the tangled vine. One arm sought for it but missed. The vine looped around his neck even as he tried to force his hands into the space below his chin. Again, too late. A loud snap momentarily vied for prominence with the sound of trampling hooves.

"Where can they be? And where is Jamie?" Marilyn asked worriedly.

"We will find them, Miss Bannon. Do not excite yourself. It does no good in this heat. You take the path to the left, and I will follow around the stables. We will meet back at the house. Is that agreeable?" the house-keeper asked.

Marilyn nodded, her eyes clouded with worry. She trudged this way and that way calling the children's names. There was no sound save that of those infernal shrieking birds. She shivered as a high-pitched squawk sounded near her. Again she called the girls. There was no answer. She followed the path to the left of the small spring. She was still some distance from the small spring but she could easily see that there was no one near. She circled back and kept calling loudly. Then, near a large bush, she spotted the multicolored scarf Rosy had worn. She picked it up with foreboding. She looked around and this time called louder. She stood quietly and thought she heard a strange sound. She spread the thick foliage near her and peered downward. There stood the huddled forms of Nessie and Rosy. Two pairs of eyes looked up fearfully.

"Why did you not answer me?" she asked quietly. "I have been looking for you."

Silence.

"Come, we must get back to the house. It is near the dinner hour."

Neither child moved. Marilyn bent down and looked closer at the children. Nessie was fearful. Rosy, usually the bright, inquisitive one, stared straight ahead, eyes dull and unseeing. Small fingers of panic gripped Marilyn's stomach. She bent down on her knees and peered at the child. "Rosy, what is it? What is wrong?" She looked at Nessie. "Tell me," she demanded. Silence. Gently she moved Nessie out of the way. It looked as though the child had been covering the small, huddled form of Rosy protectively. *Protecting her from what?* she wondered. She picked Rosy up carefully and carried her out of the dense undergrowth and into the brilliant sunshine. She placed the child gently on the ground and looked at her carefully. There was something wrong with the child. She appeared dazed. She waved her hand before the child's eyes. There was no response at all. Again the fingers of panic took hold of Marilyn. A horrible thought was creeping into her brain. No, no, she rejected the idea. Jamie would not do such a thing. Would he? Marilyn looked at Nessie. "Tell me, did Rosy fall?" she asked.

"No fall," the child said clearly.

In her heart Marilyn knew the child did not fall. She had not needed the words of Nessie to tell her this. "Nessie! Go at once and fetch Elena." The child did not move. "Nessie, you hear me. Go at once!"

"No get Elena. You take care of Rosy," the child pleaded.

Marilyn looked at the mutinous child and nodded. Tenderly she stroked the springy, black curls of the child's head. Marilyn looked up. "Nessie, I must be truthful with you. I do not know what to do for Rosy. Can you go to the stable and bring me my horse? I will take Rosy to her mother on Mr. Rivera's plantation. You too, child. I am also going to return you to your parents. This plantation is no longer safe for you. Can you do it, Nessie? Can you bring the horse?"

"I will do it, Miss Bannon," the child said quietly.

"Then hurry, child! Run!"

For what seemed like hours Marilyn sat in the small clearing, stroking the child's head and crooning softly to her. At last she looked up to see Nessie leading not one, but two horses into the clearing.

"You did say I could go too, yes, Miss Bannon?" she pleaded. Marilyn nodded. She helped Nessie mount one horse and then with a few mighty heaves she had Rosy on the back of the other. Marilyn hitched her skirts up and leaped on it too. The shock of what she had just accomplished made her smile. She had done it better than any man she had ever seen. She prodded the staid mare into a trot and kept a tight hold on Rosy.

Marilyn's mind raced. Should she go to Sebastian or should she go directly to the child's mother? She decided to go to the child's mother. What could Sebastian do? The child needed her mother.

Within one hour she had ridden into the clearing that housed the Indians on Sebastian's plantation. As before, the women came from all directions, but there was no sign or word from any of them. Gradually the crowd thinned before the determined strides of a tall Indian woman who approached from the rear. She looked at the two children and reached up with long arms to take Rosy from Marilyn's arms. Gently she held the child against her thin chest and cradled the small dark head in her hands. Tears fell from her eyes as she held the child. The jet-black, tear-filled eyes looked into the face of her child. She saw but she did not believe.

A giant of a man stepped forward and reached down to take the child from her mother's arms. He must be the father, Marilyn thought. Then there was a babble of voices. Fingers pointed to the girl's leg. Marilyn watched in horror as the mother looked at the child's leg. She traced the dark rivulet of blood that was almost indistinguishable against the dark skin of the child. Slowly she lifted the child's dress and then looked at the man, who must have been her husband. She nodded slightly. The clearing suddenly became quite still. The crowd dispersed. Marilyn, alone now with Nessie, was already anticipating how Anna would be relieved to see her daughter, and took no notice of the ominous silence.

"Come, I will take you home."

The courtyard was empty. So be it. Marilyn had no wish to see Sebastian's hard, cold, jet-black eyes that looked into one's very soul. At the sound of the horse Anna came from the house. One glance at Nessie and

Anna ran down the steps, her arms outstretched. She looked hopefully at Marilyn, who nodded. "She will remain with you now. She is your daughter and she belongs with you. I am only sorry she could not be returned to you before this."

"There will be much trouble when the Baron finds out."

"You are right, Anna. There will be much trouble. But I am the one that will administer the trouble to the Baron, not the other way around. Do not fear. No one will take the child from you. You have my word on it."

Marilyn bent over and kissed the small dark face. "Mind you take as good care of your mama as you did me," she admonished the small girl. The child nodded soberly. With a wave of the hand, Marilyn rode from the clearing. She did not see or hear the horse that carried Sebastian into the courtyard from the opposite side. Nor did she see the dark eyes gaze longingly at her retreating back. Nor did she hear the words that the housekeeper spoke to Sebastian of the golden girl with the tear-filled eyes and of the kiss she had given oh so tenderly to her little Nessie. "It would be a lucky man who could share a kiss with such a golden girl," the housekeeper said happily as she cuddled the child in her arms.

Back at the "Tree," Marilyn watched Elena as she paced up and down on the huge veranda. I will have to tell her and face the anger, Marilyn thought. Quickly she mounted the steps and told of the happenings of the past hours. Elena nodded wearily as she fingered a mutilated head from one of the toy soldiers. "There was nothing else you could do, Miss Bannon. Have you seen Jamie?" At Marilyn's negative headshake the housekeeper resumed her pacing. "He has never been gone this long. The stable boys tell me he took one of the horses —not his own—and said he was going for a ride. I fear that something has happened to him. If it has not, then there will be trouble before tomorrow. This is one day that Sebastian Rivera will not be able to hold his Indians in check. Before the night has passed there will be a death in the jungle," the housekeeper said ominously.

After bathing later that afternoon Marilyn dressed and suddenly found she was ravenous, but dinner was a trying affair. Once the food was placed before her she found she could eat nothing. She pushed the food around on her plate and nibbled on a piece of succulent guava. She asked Elena for black coffee and sat on the veranda in the deepening dusk. Savoring each mouthful of coffee, she watched the bright torches of the men as they searched the jungle for Jamie. One cup led to a second and a third. She was about to start her fourth cup of coffee when she noticed the silence. She watched as a single file of Indians paraded up to the house. In answer to their timid summons Elena emerged from the depths of the casa. Both women watched as the men placed Jamie's body on the veranda floor. They stood erect, showing no emotion on their dark-skinned faces.

Elena knelt and looked at the still face of Jamie in the torchlight. At a few gutteral words from one of the Indians, Elena looked at the neck of the once handsome lad. Her face impassive, she tersely issued instructions and the men carried Jamie's body into the house.

"I'll come with you, Elena."

"No," came the sharp answer, which then softened. "I shall do what needs to be done."

Marilyn retreated a few steps. The tightening in her breast became a strangulating knot in her constricted throat. Admiration for Elena's courage and pity for poor Jamie, as well as outrage at his transgression became a jumble within her.

Left alone with Jamie's still form, Elena began the morbid task of readying the body for its last resting place. Thoughts of tasks which needed doing clouded her reactions to the task at hand. Call Father John, locate the Baron, have the men prepare the grave . . . the grave . . . It would be in the small clearing behind the house which served as a cemetery. Jamie would be next to the mother whom he never knew.

Tenderly she bent to wash his face. Years of loving welled up in her throat. Loving Jamie had filled her life —brought meaning to it. Now it was over, quenched by the harshness of his death.

Her task complete, she stood beside the bedstead looking down at Jamie. In repose, the resemblance to Carlyle was astounding. Her mind spit out the name "Carlyle." His deceit was the cause of this. He could never admit to himself the fact of Jamie's disability. He had always insisted Jamie be treated as a man and she had tried to comply. But deep in her heart she knew he was wrong. Within Jamie's manlike body lived the mind of a small boy. Nothing could ever change that.

Elena's duties ended, she gathered up the washbowl and urn. As she turned to leave she once more glanced at the body, her mind still racing with the thought of the Baron.

Slowly she approached the still form and placed a tender kiss on the cold brow.

"Soon," she whispered softly, "soon, Jamie, I shall witness the end of your father's cruel reign. His kingdom will fall to pieces about him, and he will be nothing but an empty shell. And I, Jamie, your Elena, will do all I can to hasten that end. When it arrives I will contrive a way to be a part of it. When this comes to pass, I shall revel in the victory as I once reveled in his arms."

# 13

Carl looked at the beautiful face of Alicia as she lay in sleep and silently cursed himself and the event that had placed his beloved in this position. True, she was recovering rapidly and *that* should be all that mattered,

but somehow it wasn't. It was all his own fault. He really couldn't blame his father. If he had been a man he
would have stood up to him, father or not. He had been
weak-kneed and a coward. When he had finally learned
of his father's dubious business ventures and the way he
had cheated all those with whom he had dealt, *then* was
the time to have stood up and been counted. The fact
that he did not was what placed him in the position he
was in now. And when he had found out that the Baron
had even cheated Alicia's poor, addled father, he should
have taken matters into his own hands. That dear Alicia
and her mother did not blame Carl at all was a miracle
in itself. He would work the rest of his life to make
amends to them for his father's wrongdoing. With the
aid of Sebastian Rivera he would succeed. He was sure
of it. He looked with loving eyes at the slender girl. She
had been so firm and so honest with him. She had said
she did not care if they were penniless and he had to
work in the jungles—as long as they were together. She
had said she loved him with every fiber in her body and
all she wanted to do was to give him strong sons and
daughters to love him as she did. She had no bitter feelings about any of what had gone on before. True, her
papa was dead, and they were almost destitute, but she
had said that God would provide for them. She had even
pleaded with Carl to return to the Baron, if not to stay,
to at least make his peace with him. After all he would
be their children's grandfather.

Feeling the sudden need to touch his beloved, Carl
reached down and clasped her hand. Alicia opened her
eyes and smiled.

"My darling, what is it? You looked troubled."

Carl returned her smile. "I was just wondering how I
would ever get along in this world without you. I shall
thank God every night for the fates that brought us together."

Alicia smiled a soft smile and whispered, "You are
my lover for all time. In this world as well as the next.
We shall be so happy, my love. I will devote my life to
making you happy. There is only one thing that shall

mar the perfection of our happiness together, Carl, and you know what you must do. I couldn't bear it if you were to remain at odds with your father. Hush, my darling, listen to me. You must at least try. If your father is still adamant then you and I will at least know that we have tried. That is all I ask. That is all I shall ever ask of you. Now, Carl, I want you to promise me."

Her face looked up at him so longingly that he knew he could deny her nothing. "Very well, I promise," he smiled. "But I warn you it will do no good. My father is a strong-willed man. He feels I have failed him."

Alicia nodded. "He needs you, Carl, whether he knows it or not. It will be up to you to try and convince him that you also need him."

"Alicia, my darling, I will need no one but you for the rest of my days." Alicia raised her head slightly to receive the loving kiss that Carl bent to give her. Both lovers smiled happily into each other's eyes.

## 14

Marilyn grew more uneasy as the days progressed. Everywhere she walked the Baron was close behind her muttering drunkenly, a whiskey bottle clutched in his hand. It was almost like a parade, Marilyn thought. She at the lead and the Baron behind, followed, in turn, by Elena. Thank goodness Moriah was no longer at the "Tree"! Marilyn had removed her to her mother at Sebastian's plantation the day after she had brought Nessie and Rosy.

It was the third day, or perhaps the fourth, after Jamie had been laid to rest. Marilyn was attempting to ignore the heat by sitting quietly on the wide veranda.

However, the Baron chose to seat himself opposite her and started a tirade that had become quite familiar. "It is your fault that I no longer have sons, you . . . you . . . *you* did this," he said drunkenly. "You are the cause of it all." The once steely gray eyes were now lackluster and watery, with a fanatical cast. The lids hung heavy, as if they had weights attached. Marilyn gazed back disinterestedly and was about to answer in kind but decided against it. She had stated her case days before, and the Baron had turned a deaf ear. Instead, she looked at the caricature of the man in front of her.

"I will be leaving here on the next sailing, Baron. You will be rid of me. My lawyers will be in touch with you and will handle my affairs," she said, getting up from the bamboo chair. Her heart was heavy and she felt as if she had aged a lifetime in the last several months.

"Now that you have ruined all that I hold dear in this world, you plan to run out, is that it?" the Baron shouted in a slurred voice. "You have ruined me. I will never be able to hold up my head again in town. You have done this to me—you and that bastard Rivera. But I will mend all that."—The whiskey bottle rose to his lips —"I will settle my own debts in my own way. You shall pay for what you have done to me and so shall Rivera."

Suddenly Marilyn looked out across the veranda railing and saw Carl approach. The Baron spied him at the same time.

"If it isn't my son, the fop," he said thickly. "Have you come to gloat at your father? And where is that twit that you are so enamored of? Why do you not answer me?"

Carl looked longingly at his father. He felt his heart grow heavy at the sight of his father.

"No, sir, I have not come to gloat. I came to tell you that if you should ever need me I will not be far away."

"Need you? I need no man," the Baron roared, his face darkening in rage. "Leave my sight. As long as you remain with that twit you are not welcome in this casa."

At first Carl seemed to shrink before this rejection.

Suddenly his back straightened. He turned to Marilyn and said, "This is not a fit place for a woman of breeding or culture. I suggest that you return to your native New England. There is danger"—he looked at his father —"in malevolence."

Marilyn looked with fearful eyes at the Baron, who stood as if carved from marble, the fanatical light shining from his eyes to Carl. A chill rippled up Marilyn's spine at the thought of the remembered words, "I will settle my own debts and in my own way." She had no doubt in her mind that the Baron meant to harm her. No, she corrected, *he meant to kill her*. She was sure of it. And so was Elena. That was why she followed the Baron so closely. Marilyn had long since reached the conclusion that she had to leave. She would pack her things, go to Mrs. Quince's, and there she would remain till it was time for the sailing. She watched Carl ride off and again looked at the Baron. The eyes were once more steely and cold. They were filled with hate and malice. She let the same feeling creep into her own eyes. She held his stare boldly and he was the first to lower his eyes.

As she hastily packed her trunks, Marilyn glanced around the room that had been her home for . . . for . . . how long *had* it been? She shrugged; it had never been home. So why did it matter? She would take a last ride around the plantation. By now the Baron should have fallen into a drunken stupor, and it would be safe to ride. One of Mrs. Quince's Indians could come for her trunks. Quickly, before she could change her mind, she left the room.

Marilyn saddled the big gray effortlessly. She looked around the lush clearing at the heavy, emerald-green foliage. A strong wind whipped the long fronds, turning them upwards. The brilliant sun made dappled patterns on the pebbles at her feet. The gray snorted his impatience to be on his way. Marilyn gave him his head and rode into the warm air. Her thoughts leaped about, nimbly as her long hair in the breeze. She was going riding for the day. She would stop at noon and rest during the worst of the day's heat. As had Carl, she had to get away from the malicious, vengeful eyes of the Baron. He had said that this was not the place for her. He then had ridden back to his lovely Alicia. Marilyn marveled at the sudden change in Carl. *He positively blooms,* she smiled to herself. It must be a magnificent feeling to be so in love, she murmured to herself.

Carefully she picked her way over the strewn jungle vines. She did not want to have the same thing happen to her that had happened to Jamie. Thoughts of Jamie that she had fought to keep from her mind arose again. Here, alone, she could let them surface and examine them in the bright light of the day. Jamie had been ill. He had the mind of a child. Elena had explained Jamie's life in its entirety in a few short sentences. Not a very fitting epitaph, she felt. It was over; there was nothing she could do now. When she got to Mrs. Quince's plantation this evening she was going to send off a letter to her solicitors in New England. This way everything would be legal. A sudden depression settled over her like a mantle. She would miss Mrs. Quince and, yes, she would miss Sebastian. There was a time when she had thought that there could be some romantic feeling between them. Sebastian himself had made it abundantly clear that such was not to be the case. Evidently he preferred his women black-haired and warm-skinned. Her very blondness must repel him. Well, she thought sadly, soon she would no longer be around to annoy him. Her heart skipped a beat at the thought. Suddenly she felt lightheaded. Was that a drop of rain? She looked upward; there were dark, ominous clouds to the west. She had been riding for some time. The jungle heat was quite oppressive. She would have to find shelter somewhere. She spurred the horse faster as the clouds advanced. It looked as though it was going to be one of those storms that Elena had warned her about. She had gone off the trail in her panic at seeing the dark clouds. She took note of the strange terrain and knew immediately that she was lost. The clouds were advancing rapidly and she spurred the horse on faster. Suddenly, to her right the stark outlines of a building appeared. She reined in the horse before the decaying remains of a plantation. The jungle had advanced and smothered the darkened, charred beams of the once luxurious building. Now it was probably full of snakes, rodents, and other jungle creatures. No matter, she needed a place in which to shelter. There was no door to shut off the front entrance, so she led the big gray into a large, empty room, picking up a stout stick that lay on the wide veranda to use in case of snakes. She wished she had a candle. The bright sun of a few moments ago was now totally hidden behind dark clouds. A vicious roll of thunder split the air as a bolt of lightning zig-zagged across the sky. She shuddered. In the brief illumination she had seen what must be a crate in the far corner of the room. She advanced slowly, her hands outstretched to feel for it. When she came in contact with the crate, she sat down carefully, the stout stick clasped securely in her hands. She sat quietly for close to two hours. The storm was over as quickly as it had begun. The sun invaded the old plantation and Marilyn looked about at the large room. It almost looked like the "Tree." Could this then be the original plantation?

She then wandered from room to room; the ruin was an exact duplicate of the "Tree."

A sense of unease prickled her skin. From what she had observed of the true nature of the Baron of late, she could well believe Mr. Quinton's bold declarations. Immediately Marilyn pushed the idea aside. Although she had not given excessive thought to Mr. Quinton and his hunches, the idea of patricide was so horrible she could not even contemplate it.

She took the lunch she had prepared earlier from the saddle bag and sat on the crate. She chewed thoughtfully as she let her eyes roam the room. Something was wrong —out of place. What could possibly be out of place? She chided herself. There was no furniture in the room. For that matter there were only a few darkened beams above; most of the walls were gone. As she chewed on the soft cheese of a sandwich she again scanned her surroundings. It wasn't anything to do with the walls. She looked at the floor. No, not the floor. She looked overhead. Fire-blackened beams, but the chandelier remained intact. The dirty, grimy glass prisms still twinkled in the sunlight. She wondered why it had never been removed. That was it. That was what was wrong with the room—the great crystal globe that hung suspended from the ceiling. There was something odd about it. *What?* She stood up and craned her neck. Something must have caught her eye by chance and now that she was *trying* to find out what it was, it eluded her. She walked around the room eyeing the chandelier from different angles. She could see nothing. In her exasperation, she decided that it must have been her imagination. Shrugging, she walked back to her seat on the wooden crate. Suddenly she stood up. She pulled the crate beneath the chandelier, and climbed on top of it. By stretching she could just reach the globe. She arched her neck backward and looked carefully. There it was! When the sun hit the globe a glint of red showed. She reached her hand into the depths of the crystal globe and withdrew a red, calf-bound book. Excited, she climbed down from her perch and made haste to examine the book. It was the journal of Carlyle Newsome, Sr., the Baron's father. Now why would he hide his journal in a chandelier, she wondered? She flicked the pages. The writing was small and cramped, but she could still make out most of the words. It was amazing that the book had remained intact.

Marilyn sat upon the crate and started to read. The beginning was just a record of events on the plantation. It was dull and boring. She continued to read, however, eventually finding, "I am disappointed in my son, Carlyle. I fear it was a mistake on my part to send him away. He has returned home no better than when he left. He is a trial to me." There followed more mundane things of no great importance. Then, a later entry:

*I find with my failing health that there are a few things I must do to set matters straight before I pass on. The boy, Sebastian, is my son. A son much loved and wanted by both his mother and myself. It was she herself who would not let our secret marriage be announced. She was wise in the way of an Indian. She had said her marriage to me would only hamper my life. I fear I listened to her for I loved her dearly. She made me promise that Sebastian was never to hear from my lips that he was my son. And so he shall not. On the morrow I will ride into Manaus and leave the marriage paper with my solicitor so that on my death "The Tree of Life" will go to Sebastian Rivera, the name Rivera being his mother's family name.*

*Carlyle has disgraced himself with me. The lack of concern for human life which is displayed by him astounds me. Even after repeated warnings from me, his treatment of the Negroes and Indians did not alter. When at last he washed his hands in the blood of another human being and felt justification was ample, I could bear it no longer. That is when I disclaimed Carlyle as my son and I am much saddened.*

*My hopes for the continuation of my personal ideals and, indeed, my hopes for Brazil rest with Sebastian. I trust and believe his mother will raise him with an eye well trained to recognize human suffering. My old friend, Farleigh Mallard, who knows of this truth, has told me he can see qualities in my young son which bear grounds for my hopes. The speculation concerning Sebastian and his mother and their relationship to old Farleigh make my old friend mirthful. People naturally assume, since my wife acted as chatelaine at Farleigh's plantation, Regalo Verdad, that he is Sebastian's father.*

*My appointment with Carlyle this evening is for the purpose of informing him of these facts. Any reprisals he wishes to make I will deal with myself!*

*Upon my passing, should you, dear Sebastian, ever find this journal I want you to know that I loved you as only a father can love a son. As much as I loved your mother. You are my flesh. The flesh born of my love and the love of your mother. I have watched you grow from a child to a young man. I have watched you overcome any and all obstacles that met your path. For this, my son, I am proud of you. I ached to hold you and let you know that I was your father. What is passed is passed. Now it is my turn to make amends.*

Startled, Marilyn looked up from her deep absorption in the journal. She thought she had heard a sound. Listening carefully, she decided it was probably some jungle creature.

She turned to her reading again, although there was little more to read:

*At last my dearest wish is to come true. Sebastian will be my heir, even though my youngest son. I think I have made my decision honestly and fairly. Upon my last visit to the doctor's he advised me that death is near at hand. I only hope the grim reaper can hold off one more day. If not, then Carlyle will inherit the "Tree," and Sebastian will never know the truth.*

The journal ended here. Carefully, Marilyn looked through the remaining pages. They were all blank. So the old Baron must have died before he could set the records straight. Or someone helped him into the path of the grim reaper. There was that noise again!

Marilyn sat still and listened. She heard it again. Suddenly she saw a form in the doorway. The sun was in her eyes, preventing her from seeing the man's identity. The form advanced into the room, a revolver in his hand. It was the Baron. Marilyn gasped.

"Did you follow me here? What is it you want?"

"I did follow you here, and, yes, I want something. I

want what you are holding. Too long I have searched
for that journal. I have never felt safe since I knew of its
existence. Give it to me," he demanded imperiously.
Suddenly Marilyn knew Mr. Quinton's apprehensions
were not unfounded.

"No," Marilyn shouted. "Sebastian is the owner of
this book. It was written for him to see. Your father
wanted him to read it. I shall not surrender it to you as
long as I am alive."

"Then I shall take it from you in death," the Baron
said coldly, pointing the revolver at her.

Marilyn believed him. Suddenly she raised her arm
and threw the small, red leather journal through the
open doorway into the lush growth of the jungle. The
Baron, taken momentarily off-guard, looked in the
direction of the flying book. Quickly Marilyn reached
for the stout stick which lay at her feet. She brought it
up with a force she did not know she possessed. She
knocked the revolver from the Baron's hand. He looked
at her with such rage that his very eyes seemed to pop
from his head. His face contorted, and his complexion
changed from its florid red to purple. He could not get
his breath. Something was seriously wrong with the man.
Marilyn watched in horror as he fell to the floor. He is
having a stroke, Marilyn thought. I must get help.

She led the placid gray from the room and followed
the path that the Baron's horse had taken. Once she
came to the well-marked trails, she found that she was
closer to Sebastian's plantation than to the "Tree." She
spurred the horse on and rode into the courtyard as if all
of hell were on her trail. She leaped from the horse and
cried out for Sebastian. He came immediately, responding to the urgency of her shout.

Quickly she told him of the Baron's apparent stroke,
carefully omitting mention of the journal left Sebastian
by his father. There would be time for that later. Sebastian summoned his foreman and instructed him to follow
them with a wagon.

Marilyn mounted the gray and they rode back to the

deserted, burned-out plantation of Sebastian's father.

While the men carefully lowered the still form of the Baron into the wagon, Marilyn carefully searched the dense undergrowth for the small red journal. She heaved a sigh of relief as her hands touched the dry, cracked leather. She held the book close to her as she looked up in time to see the wagon leave.

Once again she mounted her horse and sat looking at the smooth-faced Sebastian. Jet eyes gazed back at her.

"I want to thank you for helping," Marilyn said crisply as she watched for some sign of emotion to cross the face of the man she loved—and she did love him. She had loved him before she knew of his legitimacy. That did not matter to her. And it did not matter to her that he had a kept woman in his townhouse. All that mattered to her was that she loved him.

Sebastian looked at the girl and winced inwardly. She had come to him for help and she had called him Sebastian. He had been a fool to think it meant something. All she wanted was his help. He loved this golden girl whose presence lit up the very jungle. He was at a loss as to what to say to her who made his blood run first hot then cold. He wanted her, for now, for tomorrow, for the next day, and for every day of his life. Evidently she did not think a bastard good enough for her. *Be careful, Sebastian, that no sign escapes you. Do not let her see that you care. This way she can't hurt you outwardly. Only inwardly,* he thought bitterly, and there he was wounded to the quick. Boldly he matched her look. "Then, Miss Bannon, if there is no further need of me, I will return to my plantation. If ever you find yourself in dire circumstances feel free to call on me," he said coldly.

"Thank you, Mr. Rivera," she said, matching his tone for coldness. "However, I doubt that the time will come. I have decided to return to New England." She felt physically ill with the announcement and suddenly regretted the words. She did not want to return to New England. She wanted to remain here in Brazil—even if only to catch a glance of his dear face before her and perhaps to feel his arms around her at the carnival once a year.

At her words, Sebastian felt that the world would drop from under him. He was speechless.

Marilyn held out her hand. "Take it. This is yours, or at least it was meant for you. I read it. I am sorry for that. At the time I didn't realize the nature of the journal. I almost died for this book, Mr. Rivera. I give you your life now, and," she said sadly, "I hope it comforts you!" Quickly she reined in the gray and spurred him into a full gallop. Tears flowed unbidden down her cheeks. "Damn the man! Damn the man!" she shouted when out of earshot.

The wagon bearing the still Baron creaked its way up the drive to the front of the casa. Elena, hearing its approach, came to the entranceway, her expression apprehensive.

When Jesus, lifted the Baron from the wagon, Elena came to life. She rushed to the scene and made a hasty inquiry. She then rushed back into the house to ready the Baron's bed, her thoughts in turmoil.

Days passed, the Baron hovering on the brink of death. Elena remained at his side, her vigil constant. Marilyn returned to help in any way she could, preparing meals, doing laundry, seeing to all the necessary activities in the casa.

Several times the Baron's foreman came to inquire about the state of the Baron's health. More than once a bevy of Negroes and Indians came to sit at the edge of the clearing adjacent to the casa, and toward morning they would break into a melancholy dirge which depressed Marilyn to her very soul.

"They sing like that when they believe their master is dying." At Marilyn's incredulous look Elena smiled sadly. "Yes, I know. All the injustices heaped upon them, the poverty, the slavery . . . Yet, he is their master and they do respect him, if not love him. One cannot easily instill love, Miss Bannon." Elena's eyes were sad,

but something glowed from within, something which tee-
tered between dread and contentment.

The days passed, with the Baron miraculously gaining
more strength each day, although the doctor said he
would remain permanently paralyzed on his left side.
Elena seemed to take great heart from the doctor's announcement, and the dread Marilyn had witnessed in
the housekeeper's eyes diminished to a barely visible
trace. Once again Marilyn's thoughts returned to packing her trunks and leaving the "Tree" and Brazil. On the
morning of her departure she entered the Baron's room
for the last time.

He was propped up on his chaise lounge, denying
himself the comfort of his bed. A good sign, thought
Marilyn; the old stubborness was returning, an indica-
tion that his health was on the mend.

He appeared to have aged since his attack. The lines
in his face were deeper, more pronounced, although his
eyes were alive, their glitter returned. He was clean-
shaven, save for his attractive moustache, Elena having
demonstrated her skill with the razor. The deep burgundy silk of his dressing gown made his face paler than
usual, and when he turned his head to see her, she witnessed the ravages the stroke had wrought on him. His
left eyelid drooped, as did the left corner of his mouth,
and his left arm was flung across him. Marilyn felt
slightly revolted at the paleness of his lifeless hand.

When he turned to greet her, a small lopsided grin on
his mouth marred the handsomeness that was once his.

"It seems I have you to thank for my life. I am
ashamed to say it was more than I would have done for
you." His speech was slurred, the vowels and consonants
barely recognizable. The Baron did not seem to notice.

"No thanks are necessary, sir. It was what anyone
would do for a fellow human being." He seemed to be
about to speak again, but Marilyn felt she would spare
him this discomfort. "You needn't worry, Mr. Newsome. I'm leaving for New England after a short stay
with Mrs. Quince. I shall make no demands on you as

to an accounting of the plantation. You see, in all truth, I have given your father's journal to your brother, Mr. Rivera. Now it is up to him to decide how the "Tree" is to be managed. He is a good and honest man, and I feel certain he will be most fair with you."

"I'm sure he will," the Baron struggled to say.

"Good-bye, Mr. Newsome, Baron."

At the sound of the title of respect, the invalid's face brightened. "Good-bye, Miss Bannon."

As Marilyn left the room she found Elena standing outside the door, apparently reluctant to leave her patient. "He seems much better, Elena, no doubt due to your efficient nursing."

"Yes, he does. I hope for further improvements. His temper, as well as his health, seems to be enjoying a speedy recovery."

"I'll be leaving shortly, Elena," Marilyn said quietly. "I hope you will always consider me your friend, as I will you."

"I am your friend, Miss Bannon. I'd like to apologize for my demeanor when you first arrived."

Marilyn put up a hand to still Elena's words.

"Please, Elena. We have gone through too much together to make words necessary." Marilyn embraced the tall slim form of the housekeeper and hurried away to see to her packing.

Elena entered the sick room to see about fresh water and to inquire of the Baron's appetite. He was lying quite still on the chaise and Elena felt the interview with Marilyn had tired him, for he had fallen asleep. As she was closing the drapes against the glare of the morning sun she heard him stir. In a thick speech he began to berate her.

"Skinny old crow. You make me ill with your black dresses and tightly coiled hair," he managed to sputter.

Elena turned abruptly, visibly shaken by the scathing words. The Baron was unrelenting. "Get yourself down to the clearing and send me up some young beautiful girls to dress my room. I do not want to be reminded of age, and you, Elena, do just that. How old are you now? Thirty-five? Too old for my tastes. But I can remember when you were young, Elena—young and beautiful." His eyes glittered in the way that always made her cringe with guilt and memories best forgotten.

She said nothing but quietly left the room. As she closed the door she heard him shouting in a voice that lacked its previous timbre, "Hag, old crow . . ."

Elena passed Marilyn in the hall. She swept by with unseeing determination that made the younger girl study her curiously. With a shrug, Marilyn proceeded out to the wide veranda where the men were to bring the wagon to meet her.

A few moments later Elena marched back to the Baron's room, a startling transformation in her appearance. She had removed the somber black dress in favor of the low-slung skirt and short, brightly colored bolero which was common to the native Indian. Time had dealt with Elena kindly. Her slim torso was as graceful as a girl's, and her unbound breasts were still high and softly rounded beneath the light fabric of her bolero. She paused for an instant before opening the door. With an unhurried gesture, she loosened the pins which held her wealth of silky black hair and shook it free till the length of it dropped to below her waist. Quietly, softly, she opened the door. She took two steps into the dim room and in a throaty whisper called him by a name which was only known between the two of them.

He turned to her, as though in a dream, and wondered indeed if he were dreaming. She stood there, still, in the half-light of the room, with a secret smile upon her lips, inviting him, a slim arm raised in greeting.

To his eyes she was as beautiful as she had ever been in youth. Creamy tan skin which tempted a man's hand to graze its surface. Supple, clean, unhindered lines of figure which promised passionate supplication. She was a girl again and he . . .

His eyes looked beyond her to the mirror on his dressing stand. He could see his reflection and was shocked by what he saw. There on the chaise was an old man, a crippled old man, who could never enjoy the delights which this vision of sensuousness promised.

He understood now the devious workings of Elena's love for him, unrequited for so many years. He was immediately contrite for his past actions, particularly his recent enjoyment at watching her cringe beneath the onslaught of his insults; remorse assaulted him in the peace of his room. He knew and understood that nothing, no amount of begging, would win for him her forgiveness.

She would remain by his side, a servant, never more a lover. And in remaining by his side she would mete out the cruelest of punishments ever inflicted upon a man. She would taunt him with her loveliness while her attitude would be that of a menial. She would accept his angers with a quiet smile and do his bidding. All the while, joy would sing within her. She would have him to herself and he would want her. This was to be his punishment, and had ever a woman found such a divine revenge!

His face contorted as he tried to speak. "Why?" came the slurred question.

Elena drew herself to full height, a zealous light burning in her eyes. She looked at him for a long moment before answering his question. Finally she spoke, and her words cut him to the quick as he realized their full import.

"For Jamie," came the simple reply.

While the Baron was grasping at the intent of her words, Elena glanced through an opening in the drapes. She watched Sebastian ride into the front yard. Her smile widened and a spark of pleasure for Marilyn leaped within her.

In his mind's eye, Sebastian saw himself on that day when Marilyn handed him the journal to read, her words, "I give you your life," ringing in his ears.

He had dismounted his horse and sat on the ground to read the small journal. Perplexed, he began to read. Why should Marilyn think old *Baron* Newsome's journal would give *bastard* Sebastian life? Well, he had started it, he might as well finish it. He read slowly and carefully. Then he read again, this time aloud, to the jungle, and any and all of the creatures listening to the strange, choked voice as it read incredulously still a third time. She was right; she had given him his life. What was it she had said? She had almost died for this book? That's right! His foreman had showed him the pistol. Sebastian's face drained of color and he felt dazed.

Did she mean she had saved this book for him upon the threat of her life?

He had to do something. But what? He mounted his horse and rode home to the Gift of Truth. Suddenly the exactness of the name of his plantation hit him. It had always been a mystery which old Farleigh Mallard had refrained from answering.

Marilyn would have her hands full with the sudden illness of the Baron. She wouldn't need him there, confusing her all the more. No, he would bide his time and wait for the opportunity to speak to her—when she was rested from her ordeal with the Baron, when the situation at the "Tree" had stabilized. Until then his life would be an agony, not knowing what her reaction would be to the simple things he must tell her.

Now he was here, and she was sitting on the veranda, as though she had been there all these days, waiting for him to come to her.

Quickly he strode down the veranda and came into the full view of the golden girl on the rattan chair.

She looked up, surprise written on her face and some strange light in her eyes.

"I love you," Sebastian blurted.

"Wha . . . What?" Marilyn asked, astounded at his words.

"I said I love you. I want you to marry me."

"Did you decide that before or after you read the journal?"

"I loved you before I read the journal. I thought you wouldn't marry me because of your strict New England upbringing. Once I read the journal I decided I had as much right as the next to propose to a lady."

"Don't you think it would have been fair to let the lady make the decision herself?"

It was Sebastian's turn to stammer, "Wha . . . What?"

"Why did you not let me make the decision? I have not been wrapped in cotton all my life, Mr. Rivera."

Sebastian scuffed his feet much the way small boys do. "What would you have said?" he asked anxiously.

Marilyn pretended to think. "Why, Mr. Rivera," Marilyn said primly.

"Yes?"

"Why, I would have said—It's about time!" Quickly she jumped from the chair. "Oh, Sebastian. I have loved you from the moment I set eyes on you. Did you not know that?"

Sebastian, true gallant that he was, nodded wisely and took the warm, golden girl into his arms. She felt as if she belonged there. Sebastian marveled at the warmth that came over him.

"And may all our children be as warm and wonderful as their mother," he said, looking deep into the golden eyes.

Printed in the United States
by Baker & Taylor Publisher Services